The
Worst
of Me

Kate le Vann has already had published four highly acclaimed novels for teenagers: *Tessa in Love, Things I Know About Love, Two Friends, One Summer* and *Rain*.

KATE
LE VANN

The
Worst
of Me

PICCADILLY PRESS • LONDON

*Thanks to everyone at Piccadilly Press for their
incredible patience, helpfulness, wisdom
and incredible patience.*

First published in Great Britain in 2010
by Piccadilly Press Ltd,
5 Castle Road, London NW1 8PR
www.piccadillypress.co.uk

A catalogue record for this book is available
from the British Library

ISBN: 978 1 84812 045 7

1 3 5 7 9 10 8 6 4 2

Printed in the UK by CPI Bookmarque, Croydon, CR0 4TD
Cover design by Simon Davis
Cover illustration by Susan Hellard

For my dad

They must think I'm asleep. It's only half past five, and I would be asleep if it weren't for the man telling my mum off in the next room.

I am this close, *this close* to going in and screaming at him and telling him to get out and leave us alone and never come back. I practise it in my head. I'm ready.

But my mum seems to want him here.

So I lie down and pull my quilt around me and try to hear her side of the conversation – his voice is too fuffly and mumbly.

I argued with him earlier, so I know this might be about me. In a way, I'm quite glad about that because I can see him for what he is and for some reason she can't. If she realises things are not working she's going to have to tell him to go. I'm not a kid any more and there's no way she can be okay with me being unhappy.

Suddenly my mum's voice becomes very close – she must have moved to the side of the room where we share a wall. So I can't tell what Paul says that makes her sigh and sound so sad, but her reply is perfectly clear: 'Cassidy won't be living with us forever.'

Chapter 1

You know those people who look like they know what they're doing? Confident people. The ones who don't hate their bodies, the ones who aren't afraid to say what they really think. Well, don't trust them. I know how to fake it and I can pass as one of them. But from the outside you can't tell the difference between them and me.

I think it's because there is no difference: we're all faking it.

When I'm most nervous, a kind of steel closes over my skin. I breathe really slowly and look into space with a bit of a smile as if I'm remembering something funny, or I just don't care. Like I'm maybe even looking down on the world. It's a good trick – it keeps me safe – but it has its disadvantages. Because when I'm at my most shy and terrified, when my heart's fluttery and I've forgotten how to move, and I'm wishing someone would feel sorry for me and come over and be my friend, they're probably looking at me and thinking, *That bitch is so up herself, I would never talk to her.*

But that day, someone did.

After I heard my mum saying that I wouldn't always live with her – which was true, I know, but it's just not great to find out your mum is counting down the days till you're gone – I had to get away. I lay still in my bed until I could hear the soft buzzing of his snoring, and figured that my mum would have sulked herself back to sleep, then I silently got ready to go out. I left a note on the kitchen table saying I'd gone into town: I knew they wouldn't be up before nine, they never were on Saturdays. I was out of the house by seven and the early morning chill blew straight through me because I was so tired.

I caught a bus into the city centre well before the shops opened. But there were people about, it wasn't scary, and I wasn't interested in buying anything. I just walked around, and the shops opened and the streets filled up around me. I killed time going into places I'd never been in before: I touched sleeves to feel the fabric, fanned out dresses to see their shapes, picked up shoes to look at the prices on the bottom, and told the assistants I was just looking, thanks. When I got to the cinema, I'd been walking for absolutely hours and needed to sit down. I knew I could hide there. It's not the sort of place where people from school usually go because it doesn't show the loud stupid films that everyone sees. I'd never been in there before, never even been to a cinema on my own before, but hiding is about not doing what you usually do. The film had already started when I went in, and it took my eyes a while to get used to the dark and to find out who I'd sat myself next to. It wasn't all that scary and I could see loads of people on their own. I drifted in and out of the film – it was a dark comedy with a lot of talking and I didn't really know which bits were supposed to be funny. My thoughts took over all the time, running off when something in the story reminded me of my life. But I didn't want it to end. I wanted to stay there. I watched all the credits.

Afterwards, I went into the cinema café and bought a sandwich and some coffee. It was after five o'clock and I hadn't eaten anything, so I was starving. I ate it properly, taking neat little bites and carefully using my serviette, the way you never do when you're on your own, but also sneakily brushing crumbs off my T-shirt and lap and on to the floor, worrying that I might get told off for doing that. But I didn't actually think I was being watched, if you know what I mean.

'Oi, curly!'

I'm curly – I mean, my hair is . . . but that wasn't enough to make me look. Then there was a little whistle, the kind of whistle you make through your teeth that isn't much louder than saying 'shh'.

'Curlylocks! You go to Samuel Bond's, don't you?'

Samuel Bond School: my school.

I knew who was talking before I looked. I'd been people-watching in the café, checking everyone out. There were groups of students, the boys wearing T-shirts with band names on them, the girls with pretty, short dresses and clumpy shoes; some tweed-jacketed old people talking and laughing loudly; two mums with toddlers in highchairs eating ice cream. And the four boys at the next table who didn't really look like students, and I was sure I'd seen at least one of them before. He was very tall and blond, with tanned reddish skin, and blond stubble sparkling on his chin. Rugby player shaped. Solid.

I lifted my head, taking my time to bring up my eyes to look at them. This is the kind of thing I do to pretend I'm not shy, acting bored and a bit sulky like that.

'Are you talking to me?' I said, but neutrally, not impatient or anything.

'Yeah,' said the blond boy. He smiled, as if he thought he was a bit gorgeous. Maybe he really thought that, or maybe he was faking it too. He'd have been gorgeous to a certain type of girl, the ones who like rugby players. I prefer footballers. There was one of them in the group, too – a footballer-shaped one, I mean – as tall as the blond but dark-haired and better looking. He wasn't looking at me; he was looking down and grinning, like he was embarrassed but thought it was funny. 'You just saw the film, didn't you?'

'Yes,' I said.

'We're having an argument about it now. Can you settle something for us? You know Robert? The guy who got arrested? Were Robert and the artist chick supposed to have had a thing in the past? Were they exes?'

'Sorry about him,' said the dark-haired one. 'He finds it hard to keep up with plots.'

But they all waited for my answer. When I told them what I thought, the three non-blonds did a little quiet cheer, like they'd won, then they went back to their conversation.

The dark-haired one turned back to me a minute later and said, 'Thanks, sorry to bother you.' I smiled and shrugged. Then he said, 'Is Dom right? Do you go to Samuel Bond's?'

'Yes,' I said. I looked at him. Something inside me changed . . . as if a switch had turned on. Like the way you can tell a TV is on even when the channel is dead and the picture's black.

'We haven't been there long,' he said. 'We just joined

7

the sixth form this year. I haven't seen you around.'

'She's one of the ones who goes around in little skirts,' the blond said. The other two sniggered, and I wondered if I should pretend to be offended, but I wasn't, even though it was a dodgy thing to say. I kept my eyes on the dark-haired one and raised an eyebrow. That makes me sound like I think I'm, you know, but it's all put on. Inside my heart was beating hard, although I don't know why, I was just talking to some boys in a café, not jumping out of a plane.

'D'you want to come and sit with us?' the dark-haired one asked. I froze for a moment. I might have given myself away a bit, behind the eyes.

'Maybe she wants to be alone, Joe,' one of the others said. He had thick, messy sandy-brown hair and a low, steady voice. That voice, a serious amount of stubble – nearly a beard – and the way he was leaning far back in his chair made him look a lot older than the others. I thought he probably didn't want me to sit with them.

'Well, then she'll say no,' the dark-haired one said, and he pulled over a chair from one of the tables near his. 'Come and talk to us.' He smiled. 'I'm Jonah.'

And I thought: *I already love you. Maybe you can feel it too. Isn't that stupid?* That's how I remember it happening, as everything and no big deal all at once.

You think love at first sight only happens in films, but really it doesn't happen all that much in films . . . not to girls, anyway. For boys, you usually get this thing where a gorgeous girl appears for the first time and there's hot-girl music and she's moving in slow motion with her hair blown around by wind machines and everything's lit too bright and beautiful. But that's all about looks, she's always amazing looking, and like I said, just for boys. In a chick flick, usually you're supposed to argue with the boy for the first hour and a half, only to work out what's going on ten minutes before the end.

But this. This was like: you *have* to be feeling something too. It *can't* just be happening to me. You and me are in this together, and no one else can hear what our eyes are telling each other now. It felt brave and mad holding on to his gaze like that, neither of us looking away.

They were Malton boys. Malton Road School: it's a posher school than ours but it doesn't have a sixth form. Most of them go to the sixth-form college in town, but a few choose Samuel Bond's because they like the fact that we have an old-fashioned sixth that goes back for ever and we were once a grammar school. We get about thirty of their lot a year. It's a big enough number for them to come down on us like a pack, so they don't care if they fit in. They have a rep for being snobby, but they're also a bit rich and glamorous and our girls always try to go out with their boys. That's why our boys hate them.

9

The others told me their names. The blond rugby player one was Dominic. The low-voiced stubbly one was Steve – the one who seemed older. The one I hadn't really noticed was Lewis. He had dark hair, too, but his face was ghostly white with more freckles than I've ever seen on anyone. He laughed loudly at the others' jokes but when he talked himself his voice was quiet.

They asked me questions about our school – the cafeteria, lockers, some of the teachers they had. I made them laugh. I wasn't used to making boys laugh. I wasn't used to talking to boys on my own. This is going to sound bad, but I was really glad I was alone because I knew I would have been a different person if my friends had been with me. I would have been all little and nice, and embarrassed about whether the girls thought I was trying to be fancied. I can only really do the confidence trick on my own, because I learned it to cope with being alone. That's weird, though, isn't it? Most people are better at being confident in big packs. The thing is, as far as Jonah and his friends knew, I was really that girl, the girl who was at the pictures on her own and made strangers laugh as if she didn't care what they thought of her.

The thing is, I'm not.

For a long time, I've worried about what I'm faking and what's really me, without being sure that there *is* a real me, something concrete underneath it all.

Sometimes I feel like I'm different with every single person. I get worried that I'll make a mistake and get caught out, or find myself with lots of people I'm different with all at the same time.

When you really like someone you're torn in two directions. You want them to think you're worth their time, so you lie, and try and show them the person you'd like to be. But you need them to see the real you, so you can be sure they like you for you, so you also start confessing everything and putting out your worst side, just to test them and make sure they really mean it. Then the most dangerous thing you can do happens: you stop thinking about yourself altogether – you *get over yourself* – because you're having a good time. And then who are you?

When I met Jonah I was still spending most hours of most days asking myself what was so wrong with me that had made Ian dump me. I already knew the answer: he'd found someone prettier and nicer. But I needed to feel it was something actual that I'd done, because that way I could fix myself and make things different next time, or even – I thought – get Ian back. It was hard that Ian wasn't always around now, but even harder than that was the rejection – knowing I wasn't good enough. His new girlfriend was Sophie, and I found her annoying. Not because of anything she did or was, just because she wasn't me. She had beautiful naturally-straight hair and a voice that always made her sound like she was smiling, so I never stood a chance. I had to pretend I was okay with things because Ian's sister Isobel was a close friend of mine. I couldn't really talk about it honestly to anyone else because Iso and I had the same friends.

Ian was my first boyfriend, and we'd been going out for nearly six months. If I'm being honest, that was the part of it I liked best, being a girl with a boyfriend, being part of that club where your friends talk about you as a couple. It's like your personality's not all your responsibility any more. When it was just us two alone together, we argued about only ever going to guys' films, or about hanging out too much with my mates – about a lot of stuff that seemed stupid later but wasn't much fun at the time. Sometimes we were moody with each other for no reason at all and sometimes both of us said mean things that we couldn't stop thinking about. But once I'd lost that couple status, I forgot all the bad bits and felt sorry for myself and humiliated. I'd been feeling like that for a whole summer, because it was at the end of June, just before school broke up, when Ian dumped me. That same summer, my mum turned silly over a man, so I couldn't even rely on her man-hating at Dad to make me feel better.

Then I had to go back to school and Ian was there every day, hanging around being lean and out of my league, and knowing all my secrets. I'd spent weeks imagining what I'd say if he asked me to get back with him. Sometimes I imagined myself as angry, and sometimes happy, and sometimes I just ran away. But it had all been in my head, so he had to do what I wanted. Now he was real again he could do what he liked.

He was nice. Being nice was Ian's thing. He smiled at me when he saw me, his little shy smile, where he pressed his lips together until they disappeared. He talked to me every few days. It was worst when Sophie was there, with both of them looking at me. Ian being Ian, he worked this out pretty fast, and soon he only stopped to chat when he was alone, and always about nice boring things. He made it easy to hang out with Isobel at their house. He didn't snog Sophie in the school walkways. He was just nice. It made me sad he wasn't mine any more.

'So, are we going to be allowed to talk to you at school now?' Jonah asked. 'Or tomorrow are you going to be like, "I don't know these Malton Road spods!"?' The question would have been more likely to come from me, them being sixth-formers and me being Year 11.

'Sorry,' I said, and shrugged. 'We'll have to pretend this didn't happen. I've got a reputation to maintain.'

He smiled, a great smile.

Steve, the low-voiced stubbly one, suddenly lifted

his phone and took a picture of me and Jonah. I froze, confused. 'Well, here's the proof,' he said. 'Maybe we'll use it to blackmail you.' Then everyone laughed.

When it started to get dark outside, the café seemed to magically turn into a bar. They put the lights on, which reflected all around the windows so the whole place twinkled. They turned the music up. The daytime crowd went away and a new wave of evening people with louder voices and bellowing group laughter came in their place, but we stayed through the changes, just talking, making jokes. I knew my mum would have been expecting me back because I hadn't told her where I was going. A bit after seven, I told the boys I had to leave.

'Nah, stay,' Dom said, and the others nodded. A few minutes later my phone blipped. A text from my mum asking me where I was.

'That your boyfriend?' Steve asked.

I shook my head, smiling. 'It's my mum.' I tried to keep the smile on my face, but behind it I felt depressed. Would she be angry? Why had she waited so long to text, and why hadn't she even called? The anger I'd been feeling for her earlier surged up again, taking me back to where I'd been when I walked out of the house. I didn't want to go back. I wanted to make her worry.

With friends in town, didn't realise was so late.

14

Coming home now, I texted. Then: 'Well, I could probably stay for one more drink,' I said.

At nine o' clock I stood at the bus stop with Dom and Jonah. They were getting a different bus, but said they'd wait with me till my bus came. Lewis, the quiet, freckly one, had peeled away hours ago, saying his mum would have his tea ready. Lewis was the type of boy who knows he's not cool so he doesn't try. The thing about being like that is, when you're totally outside of the being cool game it doesn't seem to matter, it's not as bad as *nearly* getting it right. People take the mick, but it's too obvious, it seems to bounce off them. Or deep down, are they feeling it? Are they embarrassed and hurt?

Steve had come with us as far as the bus stop but kept going, lighting a cigarette and then raising a non-waving hand as a wave as he walked away. In a way, I was glad because he was the one I was least sure about. I thought the others had wanted me to sit at their table, but maybe not Steve. He didn't say anything that definitely stood out as not wanting me there, he wasn't snidey or sarcastic to me, but he was more closed off than his friends. And I guess my default setting is to assume people don't like me before I know better, rather than the other way around.

I was jingly with nerves and excitement. I already knew my mum was in a bad mood: the rule was I had to prearrange where I was going with her, and today I'd just walked out. She'd texted, she knew where I was now, and that I was on my way home, but I was due some grief when I got back. And this was the first time in a long time I'd been out and not known what to expect. I was imagining school on Monday – suddenly having this pack of sixth-formers who knew who I was, Malton boys, too. Regardless of Jonah's jokes, would they speak to me? Their bus came and went, and my skin prickled with embarrassment; I don't like causing other people hassle.

'You should have got that,' I said.

'Don't be daft,' Jonah said. 'We're the ones who kept you out late. I should be taking you right to your door but . . .' He hugged his arms as if he felt the cold.

But what?

It wasn't cold, but there was that strange thinning of the air you get on warm autumn days, like the stickiness of summer has been filtered out. After half a day talking non-stop, suddenly the three of us had nothing to say to each other. We started talking about the film again, unable to find a way back into the easy joking in the café, as if Steve had taken all our funniness with him. Which was strange, because Jonah and Dom had been the ones making all the jokes.

My bus came. I stepped back to let a little old lady on it first.

'I'll see you both on Monday,' I said.

Jonah started hopping from one foot to the other. 'Should I . . . do you want me to see you home?'

'I live really close to the stop,' I said, shaking my head.

'Okay.' He sucked in his bottom lip as he nodded.

I got on the bus and found a seat on the bottom deck. The bus pulled away and I waved to them.

I told my mum I'd been with two boys from school who had seen me home.

'I didn't see them. I was looking out the window.'

'I said they didn't have to come right down the street. You know, it's such a long street, it's a cul-de-sac, I said I'd be fine. And I am fine.'

'That doesn't matter, they should have come all the way down. Who are these boys? I haven't heard you mention them. Why was it just boys? Why weren't you with any girls?'

'Jonah and Dominic. And Lewis and Steve as well, earlier. I haven't known them long. They're nice. They were at Malton Road.'

'Oh.' That seemed to satisfy my mum. Malton Road meant nice middle class boys. 'Well, you know how I feel about you being out late without telling me where you are.'

'I did tell you.'

'Beforehand.'

'We weren't sure where we were going.'

'You didn't tell me anything, though, Cass. Next time, I need to know everything. Have you eaten?'

She didn't seem all that angry. She didn't seem angry at all, even – just ticking the boxes. My muscles were tensed and hard, ready to withstand a blast of shouting. When that didn't come, I couldn't relax again, not just like that. I stopped frowning, loosened my shoulders. It felt weak and wrong.

'Where's Paul?' I said.

'He went out to meet a friend.'

I thought: *She's not going nuts at me because she's been lonely tonight.*

I thought: *They had a row. She's not that interested in me coming in late.*

I thought: *I hope he never comes back.*

I said that I'd eaten when I was out, even though I hadn't had anything since the sandwich after the film. I was happier hungry – I wanted to be thin and sexy on Monday when I saw the Malton boys again.

Chapter 2

Josette did not dislike me. Josette hardly knew me. Josette – pay close attention now! – had no negative feelings towards me.

I'm glad we sorted that out, aren't you? For some reason, though, my friends thought it needed repeating every time they talked about Josette's party, which was a lot. I was sick of everyone talking about her party because it was boring, not because I was jealous. The last thing I needed was to be reassured that Josette didn't hate me, but that didn't stop them.

Okay . . . it's never *great* to be excluded from something everyone else is going to. But I would have been fine about it without all the understanding and sensitivity and *reasons*.

'I think she just didn't think about it because you weren't there on her birthday,' Finian said. 'That was when we all started talking again. I mean, she might not even know who you are, really, you've only met her in big groups.'

'I bet if we asked her if you could come too she'd be well up for it,' Kim said.

'Well, you know she knows Sophie too, Soph'll be going, maybe she thought there'd be weirdness, not that there would be,' Isobel said. 'She doesn't know it's not like that with you and Ian.' Even though she wasn't saying so, that was the first time I realised that maybe *Isobel* was weird about me not going out with Ian any more, or thought it changed things, anyway.

'That's the point!' Finian said. 'She doesn't even know you really.'

Shut up, everyone, shut up, shut up! Did I even ask? Bloody Josette. She went to a different school – not the one Jonah and Dom had come from – but she'd gone to the same primary school as some of my mates, and they'd all met up again at a gig which just happened to be the best night of everyone's life ever, only I was out with Ian that night. We'd been arguing, as usual, about how we only did things my mates did and maybe one Saturday he could go out without having to hang out with his little sister. So we'd gone to the pictures and seen one of his stupid superhero-type films while, as luck would have it, everyone else I knew was having a better time with Josette, and I would never, ever, be able to make up for missing this one amazing night. If I sound sarcastic, it's because I'm trying to, but don't trust me: I do actually believe this crap. There'd been a lot of web chatting among them all since then, but that was the night our circle of friends had opened up and let someone new walk right into the middle, and then closed again. And somehow I hadn't made it back in time before the doors were locked.

So Josette was having a party and I wasn't invited, because . . . well, what they said, probably. I just wasn't on her mailing list because we didn't know each other. None of my friends was trying to leave me out or make me feel bad – exactly the opposite – but it was still big news and everyone's main subject of conversation. I *did* want someone to ask if I could go, but they all seemed to be offering without anyone actually doing it, and I didn't want to keep saying 'Did you ask, did you ask? What did she say?' So eventually I said, 'Nah, it's okay, if she wanted me there she'd have said. It's not really fair to put Josette on the spot.' I still hoped they would ask her anyway.

The worst thing about being lonely isn't even the way you feel, it's the fear that people will notice. That's nuts, isn't it – that loneliness should be more okay when you're on your own? During lunch break I drifted away from my mates and headed off towards the library to hide out there. It was spotting with rain outside, but I'd left my coat in the classroom and I was shivering without even feeling very cold. It was weird, like I wasn't quite inside my body. I hadn't seen the Malton guys at all, except from a distance when I'd been on my way to a French lesson and they hadn't seen me. They were looking very tall and not very real. The way I remembered talking to them now seemed to me like a story I'd retold a lot, adding more exaggeration every time till it was miles from the truth. My shirt had become untucked, the way it always did with my school skirts, and I felt scruffy and small. I'd been hoping they wouldn't notice me, but was sad when they didn't. I didn't look for them now, I just watched the raindrops making marks on my blazer and moved as quickly as I could without running. Out of the rain, through the echoy corridor, and on to the soft mossy library carpet. Safe.

And Sam.

Sam was sitting in the corner with his dark head bent over a sci-fi book, the only person I knew with hair curlier than mine. And he was the only person in there. I watched him for a moment, but that sixth sense people have, where they know they're being watched, kicked in. He looked up, and his face relaxed.

'Hey, Cass.' He put his book down.

'Hey.' I slung my bag over a chair and sat next to it. I tilted my head so I could read the writing on his bag. It said, *Resist peer pressure: all the cool kids are doing it.*

I was only friends with Sam for about a month before he came out so there was no way I knew him well enough to have stopped him. And I wouldn't time-travel back now and tell him not to. It didn't take the wind out of their sails, those people who always made his life hell, but it didn't make things worse. And you could see the difference it made for him, not having to keep the secret that they were 'right' all along, and having good comebacks when they called him names. Still, there were boys he used to talk to, sort of geeky sensitive boys – I don't mean gay, although they might have been – who you could tell had withdrawn from him a bit because they were scared of getting the same thing. Being called his boyfriend, that stuff. I worried it had made Sam lonelier, but I always think everyone is sad.

'Are you hiding from Ian?' he said. Sam talked very softly, even when he wasn't in a library.

'I'm over Ian,' I said.

Sam raised his eyebrows.

'No, honestly, I fancy other people now.'

'Which other people?'

'It's no one. Not someone who would take me seriously, anyway.'

'Do I know him?'

'He's one of the new Malton boys.'

'Right.' He narrowed one eye suspiciously. 'Do *you* know him?'

'Ha ha. We've spoken. Look, nothing's going to come of it, I just wanted you to believe me. I've moved on.'

'The new Maltesers are all right. There's one I'm hoping is gay, actually. Oh, but what if it's the same one?' He made an 'O' with his mouth and clapped his hand over it. I laughed, and wanted to shove him, jokily, but fought the urge. Sam was the least tactile person who ever lived, you could feel him tense up if you leaned against him or touched his arm.

'I probably wouldn't have less of a chance with him if he was,' I said.

'I probably wouldn't have *more* of a chance.'

The door opened and the librarian came in. She said hi to both of us, but looked at me suspiciously. Recognising me – I'd been in there before to talk at Sam for the whole lunch hour. I shuffled my chair back a bit, as if I was there to read.

'So who *are* you hiding from?' Sam said, in a whisper.

'I'm not hiding!' I said. 'I'm just tired today. Well . . .' I told him about all the party talk. I had to keep remembering to whisper, even though we were the only people in the library. I kept getting more agitated, doing impressions of my friends' voices.

'So what, it's one party!' Sam said. 'Will the boy be there?'

'Probably not. I mean, he *might*, but there's no reason he would be.'

'It'd be a waste of a new outfit, then.'

But the closer we got to Friday, the day of Josette's party, the more that thought of 'saving' a new outfit – which, by the way, I didn't own – didn't really feel like an upside. And just because it was finally about to happen, that didn't mean an end of it. There'd be the analysis – which would last at least a week – and then references to it that went on for ever, just like that concert I'd missed.

When you're in the middle of something it seems a lot bigger than it is, and although it sounds nothingy and meaningless now, it was getting to me. I wanted to sleep and stay asleep and only wake up when things were nicer: when my mum had broken up with Paul and no one could even remember being that excited about Josette's party, and some boy was waiting for me to wake up so he could ask me out. Trying to concentrate on homework was tiring me out, and I went to bed early and woke up with only just enough time to get ready and had to go to classes unprepared and feeling thick.

I was paired up with my friend Dee in English – we were once best friends, when we were really little, but had drifted quite a bit in the last few years. We hadn't fallen out or anything, just made other friends that we saw more of. It was great getting some time to talk to just her again, on her own. We were supposed to be writing a modern version of a scene from *Wuthering Heights* as a read-aloud play and halfway through the class, Dee was asking me what I thought about a bit with a grave and I was trying to bluff, and she said, 'Why do I get the feeling you haven't read this?'

'Well, the thing about that is . . .'

'Ah, come on, Cass, *naugh-tee!*' Her eyes flashed with humour. Dee had this way of telling me off and making me feel better at the same time, I'd forgotten that about her. She always looked like she was trying not to laugh. This time she really *was* trying not to laugh: she explained the plot to me and the fact that I seemed to have confused it with *Jane Eyre*, which I also hadn't read but had seen the film of. We both cracked up.

'What's up? Have you been having too much fun to stay in and read?'

I gave a long sigh. 'I wish!'

She looked up from her book and studied my face. 'Oh. You know what, a few of us are going to the pictures Saturday evening – do you fancy coming along?'

'I'd *like* to, yeah.' I was happy to be asked. I didn't think my mum would be mad about the idea after my

26

last *un*scheduled cinema visit. Even though she hadn't made a fuss when I came in, there was no way of telling she wouldn't use it against me when she wanted an excuse to be angry. 'Listen, I'll let you know if I can make it, but right now I'm not sure. My mum's a bit mental at the moment.'

Dee rolled her eyes. 'They don't let you become a mother unless you fail the psychological evaluation. Crap, we're supposed to have finished! Can I just write it for us?'

'Oh, I'm going to say no to that!'

She put her head down and scribbled away with a pencil for about a minute, stopping sometimes to cross things out with zig-zagged lines, filling the page. I watched as these perfect sentences came out of her head fully formed. What would I have given for a brain like that? Dee was a bit like my fairy godmother. She turned up just in time to cover for me in class, took the piss so I got over myself a bit, and made me feel like less of a social outcast. When we read out our scene, we were a bit hyper because we'd been laughing, and it stood out in the half-asleep class. Afterwards, the teacher raved about it and I sat and took the praise for someone else's talent, feeling bad about that, but grateful too.

We were walking out of class together and I heard a voice behind us – Alison Francis, not my biggest fan, or Dee's – doing an impression of us reading our scene out, giving us both stupid singy voices and making us self-deluded wannabe actresses. Her friend Mia laughed extra loud to make sure we could hear her. My ears kind of popped as if I'd put my head in water, and I felt hot and sick. Dee and I didn't turn round or look at each other, but I could sense her whole body stiffening and we stopped talking and didn't start again. We had different lessons next, and she gave a little sigh and said, 'See you later, then?' and I nodded.

I couldn't wait for the day to be over, but I wasn't mad about going home either. Paul was often back early on Thursdays; he worked at the university and had a half-day. He usually started making dinner to get brownie points with my mum. He'd also try to make conversation with me until she got back, for the same reason. I usually said I had homework to do and went straight upstairs to listen to music. But that narked him off, when he was trying to make a good impression and being ignored. He came up sometimes to see if I needed help, or ask if I minded 'nipping' to the corner shop for him to get him an onion or whatever.

Because I lived so close to the school I didn't have any excuses for taking my time getting home. There were no buses to let me down, no traffic jams or road diversions. So on Thursdays, just to stretch out the walk, I used to go to the cake shop in the row of shops next to the school, buy a sticky cream cake, and eat it messily as I walked home slowly. It made me feel a bit better, and also meant I wasn't starving when I got back – Paul was always annoyed if I came home and headed straight for the fridge on days when he was cooking.

That day I went for one of those weird round chocolate ball things with chocolate vermicelli all over it. I'd bitten into it even before I'd left the shop.

Then I saw Jonah at the empty bus stop.

'That looks nice,' he said, when I was close enough to speak to.

'What?'

'Your little cake.' He nodded at it, smiling. I almost threw it away, straight up in the air, like a little kid getting rid of the thing they've been told they're not allowed – it felt incredibly kiddy to be eating a cake. 'You don't have to look so guilty,' he said. 'You're obviously not dieting.'

I frowned at him, pretending to look slightly shocked. 'You know, there are *some* people who could be a bit offended by that.'

'No, I meant 'cause you're so slim,' Jonah said. 'Sorry, that sounds like the kind of thing one of my dad's sleazy friends would say.'

'How many sleazy friends has your dad got?'

He rolled his eyes upwards as if trying to remember

and count them. 'Er . . . two,' he said. His eyes glinted with fun.

We looked at each other. I didn't feel nervous now. I wasn't even nervous about the fact that I didn't feel nervous. I was excited, the way you are when your favourite programme is about to come on telly, and you know you're going to love every second but it's going to be over too soon.

'This is kind of a weird conversation,' Jonah said. He rocked back on his heels and grinned.

'Is it?' I said, with a kind of sigh. 'I was trying to sound normal.'

'You're not that normal,' he said.

'Oh . . . cause, you know, there are *some* people who could be a bit offended by that, too.'

'But not you.'

But I would be. If someone said it about me in school, like a girl, especially a girl, I would probably crumple up and stay in a ball until they let us go home. But his voice was low and those black coffee eyes were soft and it seemed like one of the nicest things anyone had ever said to me.

'How come you missed your bus?' I asked him. I knew it must have come and gone because there was no one else from school at the stop.

'I stayed behind to talk about changing one of my courses.'

'Really? What to what?'

'Oh, um, maths to economics.'

'Oh.'

'Yeah, it's not very interesting.'

There's a point when you're getting to know someone and you're still on the edge of them. Maybe you already know that this person is right for you, *your kind*. You can sense it: behind the words, something in you is speaking to something in them. But to get to that place where you can let go, you have to say enough of the things that other people say. And I was so desperate to get to the next stage that I almost couldn't come up with anything for this stage – it felt like a waste of time. I always, with Jonah, right from the start, felt that I was running out of time.

Jonah swallowed. 'So look, do you have to go straight home?'

Probably.

'No,' I said.

'Wanna grab a coffee?'

'Yeah.' I wrapped the chocolate ball in its paper bag and stuffed it in my rucksack, and wondered how chocolatey my mouth was. I was looking at the ground as we walked, watching our feet, perfectly in step. I thought about my legs looking sort of all right in my shoe-boots, which were quite high-heeled, and hoped he was looking at my legs, just so he could see they could look all right. He started telling me a funny story about the teacher he'd just seen, doing his voice, the way it went from really quiet to really loud. Sometimes I stopped listening to him because my head was just having a stupid conversation on its own, going, *Ooh, look at you then! You're walking down the road with Jonah as if you weren't some Year 11 kid he wouldn't look twice at. You'd better not be boring him*! But between his story and me trying to tell my head to shut up so I could *listen* to the story, we got to the coffee shop and we got to that next stage too.

'I wanted to talk to you before today,' Jonah said. 'But you were always on your own.'

'Isn't it harder to talk to people when they're with other people?' I said, trying to sound as if what he'd just said hadn't embarrassed me. *Excuse me, I couldn't help noticing you appear to have VERY FEW FRIENDS.* I thought about him seeing me alone, and how carefully I worked at seeming relaxed and confident when I was alone. Had there been moments when I forgot, when I let my guard down and looked lonely, or didn't it work at all?

He laughed. 'It's just hard to talk to you.'

'Oh.'

'It's not hard to *talk* to you. You know I don't mean *that*. I didn't know how much you'd want me charging up to you in school.'

'Quite a lot, it turns out.'

'Well, that's good to know. I may try it again. Look, for all I knew, what you said about us having to pretend last Saturday hadn't happened wasn't a joke. When you're on your own, you don't exactly look like you need rescuing.'

'I don't need rescuing,' I said. 'What *do* I look like?' It's awful how interested I was in talking about myself, but I was desperate to know what he thought of me. My heart stopped beating so all of me could concentrate on his answer.

'You look . . . like the pretty girl who's tired of everyone and needs to get away.' He sipped his coffee and I tried to think of something to say – and was too excited by the word pretty to respond to this – but he hadn't finished. 'But, you know, always a little bit sad, too. It's funny, how you're so funny when someone's talking to you but then you can look so sad.'

'I'm not all that sad, it's just the way my face looks,' I said, covering as much of it as I could with my hands and hair. But on the word 'face', my voice cracked.

'I know you don't need rescuing,' Jonah said carefully. 'But how would you feel about joining my gang, anyway? And we'll do brave and heroic things together.'

'Your gang?' I thought about Steve the slightly disapproving slightly beardy one, Lewis the slightly weird one, and wondered how Jonah's gang would feel about this invitation.

'Yeah, very exclusive gang. Membership at the moment is just me, in fact, so if you say no, that would be slightly tragic, actually. You should probably say yes just out of pity for me . . .' He raised both eyebrows.

I felt hot all over. I took a breath and let it out without speaking, just so I could make the moment last half a second longer. He was beautiful, sitting there in the late, low sunlight, his shiny hair, big arms, clever smile taking away any choice.

He leaned across the café table and kissed me. It was strange to kiss in the daylight when I hardly knew him. His neck smelled like lemon trees and his lips were endlessly soft. I felt as if I were floating. But thoughts of the grimness of the evening ahead piled into my head like bricks falling on me.

'I have to go,' I said. I must have said it a bit weirdly. *Don't be weird. Not yet. Let him like you first. Fool him a bit longer.*

'What's wrong?'

'Nothing. *Really.*' I looked up at him, trying to smile. 'I just lost track of the time. I said I'd be back by now.'

'Hey, don't look sad again. Is everything okay? I shouldn't have —'

'Everything's lovely,' I said. *Lovely?* I laughed at

34

how lame I sounded. 'It's all lovely,' I said even more goofily, trying to sound like I was making fun of myself.

'You're . . . kind of mad,' he said, grinning.

He brushed over the back of my neck, combing my hair through his fingertips. Just a little touch, it seemed to set off tiny fireworks all the way down to my ankles. I wished he was holding me. 'Okay, I'll let you go home, Cinderella. Are you doing anything tomorrow night?'

I wanted to throw my arms out and shout it: 'I'm not doing *anything* tomorrow night.'

Chapter 3

On Friday night my best friends were at the party of the year and I was kissing a boy on the other side of town. Have you ever wondered what's the point of kissing? If you think too hard about it, kissing doesn't make any sense and it's quite a disgusting idea. When it's with someone you don't really fancy it's more *weird* than disgusting, because you start thinking too much. With Ian, it had started to get difficult for me because he was older than me and we'd been going out six months and his mates must have been asking him about it because my mates were asking me about it. You know, *it*.

In fact, Ian hadn't been pressuring me about going all the way. But I had been pressuring myself, worried about whether he was getting fed up of me. I played the conversation in my mind – that's one of my worst habits, mentally rehearsing my future, but the real thing usually doesn't turn out the same way. I tested all the ways of telling him I wanted to wait till I was sixteen until I could do it without sounding uptight or clichéd, but I never said them out loud, to him. We just kissed. We held each other. Sometimes he held me tighter and sighed through his whole body and I was afraid we couldn't keep doing this for much longer. It wasn't that I didn't want to, I was just scared it would change us and scared of getting it wrong. I always thought it would happen, but we never had the conversation.

Now I was kissing a different boy, and that conversation was all over my head, interrupting my thoughts like my mum banging on the door of my room. Ian had always been around, I'd known him for years through Isobel. He was Isobel's brother, he'd been around since I was twelve – so Ian had always been knowable and safe. Jonah was all new territory. I couldn't be sure of understanding him or of being understood, and it was happening so fast. He was my first stranger: the first boy where the romance came before knowing him.

It made everything incredibly, incredibly exciting.

Well, look, I'm spoiling it for you, and how we got there isn't *the* most romantic thing you ever heard, or even anything you haven't heard before. But let me just relive it, because I was there and I can.

We'd arranged to meet near the magazines section of a

big bookshop at six. I got there really early and browsed slowly, hoping I wouldn't run out of things to look at, hoping he would actually come. Every time I looked at my watch it had moved on a single minute, as if I'd suddenly acquired the talent of being able to guess when exactly one minute had passed. I was there so long I went through the worry barrier, and got genuinely interested in an article in a film magazine about the movie I'd seen with Jonah (but not really *with* Jonah). So after stealing glances at the door for the full half hour of earliness, I didn't notice Jonah come in bang on time, and I jumped when he spoke to me, with his lips so close to my hair I could have turned around and kissed him. We'd already had that mini-snog in the café, so it would have been allowed, but this was our first real date and it seemed more important to get everything in the right order.

'How long have I got this time?' Jonah asked. I frowned at him, not understanding. 'I'm used to you running off when things get interesting,' he said. 'I just want to know in advance when I'm nearly out of time and I have to start cramming in all my best moves.'

I lifted my chin. 'You'd better start now.'

Jonah slid his flat hand lightly across my lower back. It made me feel like I belonged with him. 'Do you want to stay here for a coffee or do you fancy walking? It's still warm outside. I'd quite like to walk.'

'I'd like to walk too.'

We walked slowly. The sun was dropping low, dazzling us. I had a funny feeling, like I was cheating on Ian, even though it had been a long time since I'd done this kind of thing with him.

'How's your day been?' I asked.

'Slow. The whole week has been slow. I'm already ready for the next holiday.'

'We've hardly been back.'

'Well, it's back for you,' Jonah said. 'It's all new for me.'

'And what's the verdict? How's the new place working out for you?'

'Your teachers are all insane.'

'I could have told you that.'

'Your guys are all chippy.'

'Yeah, well . . . I think they just take a while to make their minds up about new faces,' I said.

'Maybe,' Jonah said. 'There's not much interaction, though, is there, between the, uh, various *gangs*?'

We carried on walking in silence and it wasn't awkward, but I wondered who was going to break it.

Then I blurted, 'What about our girls?'

'Your girls are good fun,' Jonah said, nodding. 'Some of them have definitely got potential.'

'Oh really! Potential for what?'

'Well, just as an example, you, I mean taking just one example, you understand . . .'

'Yeah, yeah, I understand, just as an *example* . . .'

'Well, I could see you as a long-term friend, you're definitely long-term material.' He cupped his hand in front of his eyes, shielding them from the sun, and turned towards me. I searched his face for sarcasm, but it wasn't there. That seemed somehow sweeter than a compliment about fancying me – that he'd be serious about wanting me as a friend. We'd reached the steps of the city hall and climbed up a few and sat down. 'Are you warm enough?' he said.

'Yes.'

He reached for my hand and held it. 'Your hands are cold.'

'They always are.'

'It's funny, isn't it? We've spent all our lives in this town, walking around the same streets, being alive at the same time, and we've never seen each other before. I mean, probably we've been in the same building together at the same time, like . . . WH Smith's or something . . .'

'I have actually been to WH Smith's!' I said.

'Me too!'

I had this crazy big grin on my face because he was being so silly, but he was funny about it, totally straight-faced as if he might have really meant it, this wonderment that our destinies had had us circling each other around pencil case racks and magazines long before meeting. I don't even know now how much he was joking!

'So I'm going to guess things about you,' Jonah said. 'Just on firstish impressions, and you can tell me how right I am.'

'Okay,' I said. 'Everyone likes being told things about themselves.'

Jonah knotted his fingers through mine. 'You're very independent.'

'I can be.' Had I been holding his hand too loosely? Like I wanted to get rid of it?

'You're a bit older – in your head – than your friends. You sometimes find it hard to explain exactly what you're trying to say to them because they seem to be a few chapters behind you. I don't mean, like, in school, necessarily, but in . . . things, people, what you want to do.'

'Well, I wouldn't . . .' My head seemed to empty and flood all at the same time.

'It's okay, I'll just keep going.'

'I'm sure my mates wouldn't . . .'

'You've got a strict . . . dad, I think.'

I breathed in quickly, then again, slower. 'It's . . . true and not true,' I said. 'I don't really see much of my dad any more. He's got a son, my half-brother – Nathan – and it's not that I don't want to know him, but we don't have a lot in common. He's just this eleven-year-old boy I barely know, it's kind of exactly the wrong age to want to be dragged out to restaurants with your dad's other family. I've been seeing my dad less often anyway . . . I shouldn't really be talking about this, you're going to think I'm —'

'No, it's me. I shouldn't be talking about this. I'm sorry if I've made you uncomfortable.'

'You haven't. It's all right to talk about it. But I shouldn't, because I'll make *you* uncomfortable.'

'No,' Jonah said. 'It sounds really tough. Not that your brother is a stranger or anything, but you won't be able to talk the same way with your dad that you would have before – and that's your time together. He lives with his son, he doesn't need to spend more time with him.'

I nodded, because he understood, which made me sad. The stone steps we were sitting on were starting to grow colder. I stretched my legs, pointing my toes. I could smell the fat from a chip shop and it made me feel sick and hungry at the same time.

'My mum has this boyfriend now, and he's always giving me a hard time.'

'He's the reason you had to run back home so early?'

'No, that's my mum. But he's the reason I don't *want* to go back home.'

'He's all right, though?'

I guessed he meant, was there anything really bad

happening, and there *wasn't*. Paul would never hit me or anything, or my mum, but his being there was always a lot of pressure, just his *being there* – like it was pushing me into the walls, taking all the oxygen, making a load of white noise. He was bigger than himself.

'Yeah, yeah,' I said quickly. 'He's all right. We're just two people who shouldn't have met.' I shivered.

'You're cold.'

'I'm fine,' I said, but he'd already taken off his jacket.

'You're cold and I'm not,' he said. 'But let's go somewhere.'

The somewhere we found was a little second-hand record shop. When we walked in, the emo bloke behind the cashdesk said hi to Jonah like he knew him. I was surprised: Jonah was really clean cut and quite preppy, an Abercrombie & Fitch type. I'd never been what I'd call cool. I wondered if we stuck out there. It was more of a uni hang-out, and downstairs it also sold weird vintage stuff – lamps, furniture, toys, a few clothes – and there was a café. The chairs were moulded orange plastic and on the tables there were pages from Japanese comics under perspex. The people at the next table were calmly rolling cigarettes that may have been a bit spliffy, although they weren't smoking them. We drank cappuccinos and shared a brownie, and I'd asked Jonah to talk a bit about his own family by then.

'They think they're cool and permissive,' he said, 'and I used to think they were too, but the older I get, the more I think they're a bit more traditional than I used to.'

'Or they just seem like that because there's more stuff they don't want you to do than there was before,' I said.

'Oh, I don't mean with me, I mean with the world in general. But that's a problem for you, though? Pointless rules?'

'Maybe it's just different for girls.'

'I'm sure it is,' Jonah said. 'But it's harder if it's not actually your dad telling you what to do, just someone else.'

'He's such a phoney,' I said. 'He tells me people will "call me names" if I stay out late with boys. I just find it creepy.'

'It's like he's too interested in your sex life.'

Yes, that was how I felt, but as I didn't really have one of those, I blushed and carried on.

'He's got strong ideas about how people are going to see me, morally. He's really into telling me how I'll be seen by boys, but he as good as lives with my mum now – he's got his own flat, but he's never there – and they're not married. What a hypocrite.'

'Is he some kind of God-botherer?' Jonah said.

I hadn't heard the term before. 'You mean a Christian?'

'Yeah. Any religion, really.'

'Yes, I think so. You're not, then?'

'No, we're not big on religion.'

'Your family?' I asked.

'No, everyone you met at the pictures. Me, Dom, Steve. Lewis. It's been a bit of a culture shock, in fact, coming to your school because people tended to be more of our mind back at Malton Road.'

'Why?'

'You know everyone in the sixth has to do general studies at A-level here?' he asked, and I nodded. 'We've started off with something called "study of contemporary British society" and a lot of people have been getting a bit *eager* in the debates about religion.'

'*Really?*'

Jonah shrugged. 'They set up a talkboard about it on your school intranet, you should take a look.'

'Who set it up?'

'Well, it's part of the course, so the teacher, oh, what's his name, not Bailey . . .'

'Mr Billingsley?'

'That's it, Billingsley, he set it up. We're all supposed to keep throwing ideas about, carrying on the discussion between the classes. We realised pretty early on that it was very easy to offend some people, and what with us being the new boys, we took the discussion somewhere else. We set up a Facebook group called We're All A Bit Afraid Of The Sam Bond Nutjobs, but they found out about it so we took it down.'

'Was this all pretty serious?'

'Well, that group wasn't. But yes, people have been quite seriously pissed off.'

'Maybe it's just people want to argue with you because there's that thing of our guys needing to be convinced about you lot. Like you said, they can be a bit chippy?'

'It's not that,' Jonah said. He picked some brownie crumbs off the table, where they'd been freckling a little Japanese rabbit superhero, by pressing them with his fingertips. 'I think my mates and I do feel quite strongly about this as well, to be quite honest. If you think about it, so many of the world's problems are caused by religion, religious intolerance, hatred of one religious group by another religious group – look at Palestine, Iraq, look at 9/11.'

I didn't really know much about any of these things, but I understood enough of them to agree. 'Even our own country and the Northern Ireland situation,' I said, keeping it vague because I didn't really know what that was all about.

'Exactly!' Jonah said, and I was glad the bluff worked, but felt that familiar lurch in my stomach – fear that I was trying too hard to be the person someone wanted me to be, and doing it too well.

'Are you okay?' I said suddenly. 'Are you having trouble with our guys? It's come up a couple of times now.'

'They're your friends,' Jonah said. 'I'd have to be some kind of idiot to start slagging people off in front of you.'

'They're not *all* my friends,' I said. 'Did you get on with everyone at your school?'

'True,' he said.

'But it's okay? You don't want to leave? You're not being . . .'

'What, bullied?' Jonah smiled. 'Would you hang around and stand up for me?'

'I don't mean . . .' I was afraid of having called him a wimp.

'I'm just teasing. It's all okay. It's good. And no, I don't want to leave. Quite the opposite. If anything, I've recently found a reason to want to be around the place even more.'

'What's that?' I said.

Jonah rolled his eyes. 'Come on.'

'Oh, really?' I felt my face go red. '*Really?*' I became aware of the people around us, as if the volume of their conversation had been suddenly turned up. Jonah reached across the table and held my fingertips. We both leaned forward at the same time and kissed. It happened slowly, just our lips touching, tugging, but it was intense and passionate. And when I opened my eyes, a guy at the next table said, 'Aaahhh,' and sniggered, and his girlfriend shushed him. But instead of feeling self-conscious, I felt giggly and proud.

Chapter 4

'The thing is, Cassidy, you have to respect yourself or no one is going to respect you.'

'Sorry, what's the problem here, *Paul*?'

I'd walked in the door at a little past half past ten, which was bound to be by miles the earliest of everyone I knew that night. I'd been okay about this. It had felt embarrassingly early when explaining it to Jonah, especially as all summer long the six-year-olds next door had been playing out in the street till about the same time. But I'd agreed with my mum to be home then because I was going out alone with a boy she didn't know – something I might not, incidentally, have even *told* her. I knew people who would have just said they were out with their usual mates. If I'd gone to the party and had been sure of a lift home, I would have been allowed out till midnight, like everyone else. She was always fine with someone else's parents making sure I was safe. I'd called at ten to say I was on my way home and everything was fine. *So just run this by me one more time, Paul: what is the lecture about?*

'There's no problem,' Paul said, and he seemed to make a point of relaxing his voice. 'I just think the nice thing for this boy to do would be to stick around and say hello when you came in the door.'

I blushed, imagining this situation. 'Well, I said it was best for him to go. He saw me home, right to the door. I think it's a bit early for him to meet the . . . uh . . . *parents*. I don't think I'm *that* serious about him yet.'

'All I'm *saying* is, and your mum is too afraid of upsetting you to say this, this is a very difficult age and it's best to do things properly.'

'Really, Mum, are you too afraid of upsetting me?' I could hear the way I sounded: furious, sarcastic. But while my friends were out doing the things that most teenagers got up to on Friday nights, I was getting some kind of random lesson in etiquette even after I'd followed the rules.

'All I'm saying is, if you want boys to respect you, you have to insist on doing things properly.'

'Mum,' I said again. 'Why do I seem to be in trouble? With *him*?'

'You're not in trouble, and don't call Paul *him*,' my mum said, finally joining the conversation – to defend

Paul. 'What you don't really understand, and there's no way you could, you're just a kid, is how Paul and I have sat at home worrying about you all evening and thinking about the things we ought to tell you, the things you ought to know, and now seemed as good a time as any. We just want you to be safe.'

'I *always* keep myself safe,' I said.

'Of course you always have,' Paul said. 'But it's fair to say that we know more about the stage you're going through now than you do.' Ugh, *the stage I'm going through*. I didn't even want to think about what he meant by that. 'And this boy is older than you, you said. While we were all here and you were in what I thought would be a good mood, I —'

'I *was* in a good mood . . .'

'Cass,' my mum said. 'Stop being rude to Paul. How do you think he feels?'

'I'm sorry, this is just too weird. There's nothing to talk about. I'm going to bed. At ten forty-five. Wow, what a rebellious teenager I am. I can see why *Paul* is so worried.'

My mum followed me upstairs and closed my bedroom door behind her.

'I don't understand why you're being so rude to Paul,' she said, almost whispering. 'He genuinely cares about you.' She looked pink, and I couldn't tell if she was angry or upset or just hot.

'If you have a problem, Mum, then talk to me. Don't get Paul to talk to me.'

'I didn't *get* Paul to talk to you.'

'Then don't *let* Paul talk to me. It's just so . . . *wrong*, I can't tell you! Look, you made the rules, I stuck to them, why are we even fighting?'

'We weren't!' she hissed. 'Until for some reason you went mad at Paul calmly asking you why this boy didn't come in and meet us – and okay, I realise it isn't very cool to ask him to do that, but Paul is old-fashioned. That's one of the reasons he's good for me.'

I breathed out loudly. 'Well . . . good for you, Mum.'

She rolled her eyes. 'Well, thanks, Cassidy, it's nice that you're being as miserable as you can be about me trying to be happy again.'

Too much. Guilt overload. Please exit the room before it explodes with the stuff. I didn't say a word, I just looked down at my feet until eventually she left.

I checked my phone and there were two texts from Jonah. I felt myself unwinding as I read them. Just funny things about the people he'd seen walking home, and how he thought this had to be a perfect arrangement: having a girlfriend who sent him back home in time for *Match of the Day*.

Girlfriend. Which meant I had a new boyfriend. My first – slightly wrong – thought was, *Great, now I can talk to Ian again without him thinking I'm still not over him.* My second – slightly wronger – thought was, *I wonder if this will make Ian jealous.* My third – probably sensible – thought was, *Ohmygod, I hope Jonah doesn't think I'm ignoring his texts.* I sent one back and didn't try too hard to be clever and funny, because those are the ones I always regret in the morning.

Getting over someone doesn't start when they dump you. That's when you go fast and hard in the other direction, convincing yourself that they were even more perfect than you realised and your life will never be the same again. It starts for real when you find things to be happy about that, okay, often involve them, showing them what they're missing, or that you can do fine without them. And sure, it's not good that they're still in focus, less good that the feelings are about revenge and hoping they care. But those little thrills tell you that your life has started again and fun is out there, not inside your bedroom, listening to his favourite song. You're driving this thing again. After that, you get swept up in what you're doing and never look back.

The truth is I was well swept up already, floating on a wave of adrenalin. Some of my thoughts might have been about Ian, but that was two or three thoughts out of two or three million. I lay on my bed, buzzing about my evening with Jonah, fizzing with anger about Paul and my mum. Sometimes I sighed and smiled and hugged myself, then all the happiness would crumple under doubts and panic about what was going to happen, and my face knotted into a frown. I seemed to have outgrown uncomplicated happiness. My life was too difficult for that now.

In the morning, my mum and Paul left early to go shopping, and I came downstairs to a gorgeously peaceful house. I spent some leisurely time on the computer, reading the papers for celebrity news, then sent emails to all my girls who'd gone to Josette's party, casually mentioning that I'd been out with Jonah. I also emailed Dee about going to the pictures, telling her I wasn't sure if I could go yet, but just on the offchance that I could, would it be okay if I brought a boy? Her reply came back first, saying of course I could bring a boy, and issuing a demand for more details. Then a trickle of emails came from my other friends that all focused on the same thing: our shyest friend, Kimmy, had pulled. There was surprise that I'd been on a date, and pretend-anger that I'd kept it a secret until now. I think it came as a relief to them that I hadn't spent the evening feeling left out. I emailed everyone back, reread every email I'd received and sent that day, took a deep breath and emailed Jonah.

Morning. Had fun yesterday. One of my friends – Dee, she's ace – is going to the pictures tonight and asked me along – might be quite a few people, so understand if you'd rather not. Maybe you know her brother Nashriq, he's in the sixth to, and lovely.

As soon as I'd sent it I wondered if it was too early to be asking him out. Then I read over the mail, saw that I'd spelled 'too' the wrong way (with just one 'o'), groaned and slapped my hand on my forehead. Now he'd know I was an idiot. I thought about sending another email just to correct my spelling in the one before, but knew that would be worse. If only I'd texted, 'cause then bad spelling is part of the language.

Jonah didn't reply for nearly two hours. When he did it was to say no. But not big no.

Sorry, already told lads I'd see them tonight, no chance of making pictures with your friends. But come along with us if that doesn't sound too much like punishment. We haven't really made any plans, but we usually fall into doing something decent on Saturdays. If you don't mind the blokey imbalance, I'd love you to come.

I waited until the clock had ticked on a respectable eleven minutes.

Sounds fun, but if this is more of a lads night out, don't want to cramp your style by asking stupid questions about offside rule and rating football players in terms of cuteness.

Jonah: *But would you like to come? Let that be the guide.*

55

Me: *Yes! If it's really okay?*

Jonah: *Hmm, tough choice. Night out with my best mates, or night out with my best mates and a brainy sex kitten . . .*

Even though I was on my own I hid behind my hands and peeked at that email again. I wanted to write back something self-critical but I stopped myself. What had first attracted Jonah was me being cool and collected; I had to remember not to blow it too early by falling into being girly and hopeless. I wrote back: *You make it hard to say no.*

Jonah: *Damn, I was aiming for 'impossible'. Do you want me to come and pick you up at your house or meet you somewhere further away? What's easiest?*

I leaned back from the keyboard and looked guiltily around. Would it be safe for Jonah to come to my place, or would Paul be lurking when I left the house, ready to spring out and start trying to shake hands with him?

Another email appeared: *Cassie – pizza night tonight at Iso's, what do you reckon? Unless you have another hot date! Finian xoxox*

I did! It would have been lovely to hang out with the girls when I had really juicy news for them. But sometimes it's better to make the news than to report it.

Then one more email popped into the box: *Feeling lonely. Cheer me up? Sam x*

So I wrote to Sam, taking my time. I had good things

to tell, but I didn't want to sound smug when he was blue, so I threw in a couple of my own problems, then found myself opening up about all my insecurities and worries, telling him everything I wanted to say to everyone else, all the sad stuff about my mum and dad that I was already worried I'd overhassled Jonah with, and I asked him tons of questions about how men thought. By the end of it, the email that had been supposed to make Sam feel better made me feel better: I often found a way of turning trying to be nice into being quite selfish. At the bottom, I added: *Want to hang out tonight?*

And it wasn't just being nice: I would have loved an evening with Sam. I almost *needed* to fit one in before I saw Jonah, it would help me get my head together and play things the right way. But obviously part of me was also hoping Sam would say no. He did: *There's literally no way I'm tagging along on a date where I'm not one of the romantic leads, looking like your comedy sidekick. But it's nice to be asked. As a reward I will analyse your new romance as much as you like and give you brilliant advice. Full report when you get home, please.*

I sent a short reply to Finian, turning down pizza night. It felt good to let them know I hadn't needed them after all – not to gloat, but to get back from feeling like the saddo who hadn't been invited to the best party.

But Jonah being my boyfriend wouldn't feel real until he and my friends had met. I told Jonah I'd meet him outside the shops round the corner from my house, and asked him to stay in touch by text now because I'd probably be offline for the rest of the day. Then I put the computer to sleep, having been typing solidly for two hours. I had to think of something to wear. I held off showering, too, it seemed stupid to have one too early as I'd have started to wilt by the time I left – but if I stayed in my PJs I knew my mum would come back from the shops and complain about me lazing around all day. I put some jeans and a white T-shirt on and brushed my hair back into a tight ponytail. As I heard her car coming up the drive, I put the kettle on. I didn't want to fight.

She was alone. Paul played football on Saturdays, she'd have dropped him off. She had a car full of supermarket food and I helped her in with it.

'Are you feeling better today?' she said, which made me bristle, because it seemed to say I'd been the unreasonable one the night before.

'I wasn't in a bad mood yesterday,' I said.

'Well . . .' my mum said, and then, infuriatingly, acted as if she was trying to silence herself because it would be unwise to fight with me over this, like I'd go crazy 'again'. I didn't want to fight. But there was no point making things worse.

'Well,' I said. 'I really wasn't.' And I even put some comedy sulkiness into my voice, on purpose, as if maybe there *had* been a bit of that, me being a teenager, all difficult and angry.

'It's hard for Paul to know how to talk to you,' Mum said. She made herself busy filling the fridge, and she didn't look at me once. 'He's afraid of coming on too much. He knows he's not your dad.'

'He doesn't have to try to be,' I said. My mum shoved at an overstuffed freezer drawer and the noise it made was like fingernails down a blackboard.

'Do you want to talk about this new boy?' she said.

I laughed. 'No!'

She turned away, looking hurt.

'Well what do you want to know? I told you his name, where he's from, what he looks like. That he's nice. That it's really early days!'

'I don't know how I should talk to you about boys,' she said, and sat down at the kitchen table. 'I didn't have a mother at your age. I don't know what everyone else is doing. What is everyone else doing?'

I poured her a cup of tea and sat down too. She sipped the tea quietly.

'I think they do it the same way you do,' I said. 'It's like you said, it's hard when Paul talks to me.'

'Are you seeing him again tonight?'

'Yes.'

'You haven't even asked me if you can!'

I felt the rage rising in me again. It was the way she made it like a game, and only she knew the rules. Sometimes we were grown up and talking together like friends, then in an instant things changed and I had to remember that we were not equal at all.

'You asked me if I was seeing him again tonight. I should have said that I *wanted* to see him again tonight. Will that be okay?'

'What's his name again?'

'Jonah.'

'I know that. Jonah what?'

'Jonah Brooks. Are you going to google him?' Every time I made a joke I knew she might take it the wrong way – but I kept trying, because I wanted her to loosen up.

'I probably will, actually,' she said, not making a joke, but aware that it sounded like one. The older I got, the more I understood my mum's sense of humour. She hardly ever laughed but she often said funny things, knowing they were funny to other people, and liked it when they laughed. 'Do you want to bring him round? You can sit downstairs with him, I'll stay upstairs. I won't embarrass you.'

'We're meeting up with his friends,' I said. 'I can't bring them all round here.'

'Hmm,' my mum said. 'All boys again?'

'Probably.'

'Just be careful with boys. When they're all together, they make their own rules.'

'I don't know what that means,' I said. 'What does it mean?'

She sighed, as if I was wearing her down. 'It just means, be careful.'

I was feeling triumphant when I called her later that evening. The five of us: me, Steve, Lewis and Dom, and Jonah, had opted to go to Jonah's house. A big house, on a street full of big houses, quiet outside, posh and lovely inside. We were drinking red wine with his parents while his ten-year-old sister, Lucy, made everyone laugh by insulting her big brother and doing impressions of him. Jonah's dad said he'd give me a lift home, and his mum asked if I wanted to let my mum know because she might let me stay out later.

'We'll all talk loudly in the background when she picks up,' Jonah's mum said. 'So she'll know it's true and you're safe, and not necking in a park with a bottle of alcopops.'

I must have blushed, because she said sorry and smiled even more. She wasn't very like my mum – she was warm and confident, but scary too.

My mum answered her phone and agreed to letting me stay till midnight, asking about five times if that would be okay with Jonah's dad. She sounded very timid, as if she could tell I was with posh people just from the way her phone had rung.

'Which film are you going to watch, anyway?' Jonah's dad said. 'I could let you have something that will actually change your lives, something genuinely good, you know?'

'We're always very grateful for your recommendations, Mr B,' Steve said. 'But I don't think we should watch porn when Cassidy's here.'

They all laughed, Jonah's dad the loudest. 'Don't pay any attention to him, Cassidy,' he bellowed. 'I'm talking about Godard, maybe *The Godfather*. Something that will educate these hoodies. I'm afraid you're not likely to get anything improving from them.'

'Actually, we met Cassidy at a clever film,' Jonah said.

'Go in by mistake, did you?' his dad said. He turned to me. 'You probably had to explain the plot to them.' I paused, starting to smile, while the guys exploded with laughter around me. 'You did?' Jonah's dad said. 'Ha-haaaa!'

It was nice, genuinely funny, but in some ways the friendliness was as full-on as Paul's awkward, forced strictness was at my house, and I could have done with less attention. I was relieved when the guys moved into a room they called the den, leaving the grown-ups and cute little sis behind. There was a massive telly and Blu-ray in there, and Jonah's mum had given us plates of bread and cheese, olives and ham and sausagey things to eat. There were two sofas making an L-shape in one corner. Jonah and I took one, Steve and Dom took another, and Lewis sat on the floor in front of them, leaning against their sofa. Jonah put his arm round me straight away, and maybe no one noticed or maybe no one cared. Dom put a horror film on and there was silence for the first twenty minutes. Then Steve said something funny, then Jonah said something funny, and after that they all commented most of the time. I was happy for them to talk over the film because it was really scary, and I was glad I wasn't getting a bus home.

We sneaked in a couple of cheeky little snogs at the most gory moments, but mostly we just held hands and joined in with the joking. There was a lovely mellow vibe. It made me feel like part of a long-standing couple, the way things had been at Isobel's house when Ian joined me and my mates. Better, though. These people were letting me pretend to be someone I'd never been before, someone quicker and braver and prettier and better. I even seemed to be getting away with it.

Chapter 5

'So what's with the Cinderella story?' Sam said. 'The last time I talked to you you were moping around, not being invited to the ball.'

Hmm, freaky! Jonah had called me Cinderella because I had to go home too early. This was a sign, or something. 'I know,' I said.

'These plastic chairs are really uncomfortable.'

'Yeah, sorry about that.' I'd taken Sam to the café in the record shop where Jonah and I had gone on our first proper date. 'I've only just discovered this place, I thought it was cute.' I noticed that the cake was dry and the coffee had been brought to the table already cold. Things were always worse when you recommended them to other people.

'I've been here before,' Sam said. 'With a guy I thought might be straight and confused, but wasn't: he was definitely gay. And definitely didn't want me. Did you come here with Jonah?'

'Oh, Sam,' I said. He always skimmed over his romantic failures, and if I pressed him about them, he made a joke and changed the subject. 'And yes, Jonah brought me here on Friday. I've never been in before, I thought it was just a record shop.'

'So he's a bit of an indie kid?'

'No, you definitely wouldn't say that if you saw him.'

'What is he, then?'

'Not everyone belongs to some kind of tribal category,' I said, comedy-scolding him. 'I think Jonah's really too mature to be put into —'

Sam laughed.

'All right, when I say mature, I just mean . . . he talks about real things, you know, the world, politics, not just —'

'But *you* don't!' Sam said. 'What are you talking about when he's talking about the world and politics?'

'Oh shut up!' I laughed. 'I'm *listening*. He's good for me.'

'Do you really like him? Or are you just trying to improve yourself while you're getting over Ian?'

I thought about Jonah. His sexy, gorgeous, film-star face, the way he seemed to have been designed for me to hold, to walk with, exactly the right shape and size for me. My head got light and fizzy, like lemonade sparkling in sunshine, and my lips pulled back in a smile so silly and wide that I tried to fight it.

'OK, you don't have to look so *happy*,' Sam said. 'I had about ten minutes of you being my fellow sad single friend, it's not fair.'

'You had all summer!'

He talked over me. 'I don't want to hear it. Don't tell me. But I do want to meet him. You said he's got rugger-bugger mates, though – aren't they usually homophobic? The kind of homophobic who take naked showers together, wear each others pants on their faces and call me a shirtlifter?'

'I said Dom *looked* like a rugby player, I don't know if he plays it, though. Look, Jonah's got sweary, liberal parents, they gave us wine to drink, they're the kind of people my mum's boyfriend would be terrified by. I think the one thing I can count on Jonah being is politically correct.' My phone beeped with a text. I glanced at it. Fron Jonah. I tried not to smile.

Sam rolled his eyes. 'Ughh, don't show me, don't tell me, I don't want to see it. What's he saying? Miss you already? Ooh you're such a good kisser? I heart you?'

I grinned and said nothing. He glanced at me and I rolled my eyes.

Sam laughed. 'Let me see.'

* * *

Monday morning was the next test. We were definitely a couple now, and that was never an easy thing to debut in a school setting. I was eating breakfast in the kitchen, distractedly watching telly programmes made for tiny kids. The same ad for hideous sparkly pink shoes had appeared in every single break, and its weird little jingle was starting to feel like part of my brain tissue. My mobile rang in the living room. My mum didn't seem to hear it, she was eating toast and reading the *Daily Mail*.

'How about,' said Jonah's voice, 'meeting up now-ish, and we can get each other out of our systems before we have to go into school and mostly ignore each other?'

Happy, sad, amused, confused. Oh, and lustful. But if I was going to meet Jonah before school I wasn't going to waste time getting clarification on the phone. I didn't have any make-up on yet.

'Mum, I'm gonna set off now and get in early,' I called. I drew hasty kohl lines around my eyes, then added lipstick, blotted with my fingers and rubbed the excess on my cheeks. A smudged coat of mascara. The light in the living room was flattering, it looked good enough.

My mum came in. 'How come?' she said.

'That was Isobel on the phone, she left her jotter in her locker, she hasn't done her physics homework,' I said. 'She needs to borrow my notes, so she can try and do it before first period. I'm gonna go and meet her for a coffee.'

She yawned for a long time. 'Cassie?' she said.

'Uh-huh?'

'I love you, sweetheart.'

I stopped throwing stuff in my bag so that she wouldn't think I was being dismissive or rude, but I couldn't think of anything to say. We both heard the door bang upstairs as Paul came out of the shower. I gave her what I hoped was a reassuring smile. 'I have to go,' I said, shaking my head. I didn't lie to my mum very much, and there was really no reason to lie to her that morning. I just had a feeling it'd make things easier.

Jonah had called me from the bus and I actually got to the stop before he did.

'You're always early!' he said. 'You make me worry that I'm late.' We held each other's fingertips and I stood on tiptoe to kiss him. 'So we've got half an hour,' he said, softly. 'Let's go mad with it.'

We walked down the hill to the school entrance, Jonah's arm curled around my waist and me holding his hand.

'I think I have to apologise for my dad's terrible jokes when he gave you a lift home the other night. I . . . think I must have been adopted, it's the only explanation.'

'Your dad's great,' I said. 'Both your parents are. You have no idea!'

'Everyone thinks the worst about their parents.'

I shrugged. 'Some parents don't give you much to be positive about.' I worried I sounded too dark and miserable, so I smiled. 'Yours are cool, believe me.'

We reached the school gates, and paused.

'Shall we go in?' Jonah said.

'It's not even ten to eight.'

'They let you in, though.'

'Well, not in the building.'

'Yeah, I think in the building.'

'But, we're not allowed in the building. And where would we go anyway?'

Jonah grinned. 'It's cold out here. Warm in there.'

'But . . .'

'We could lurk inside the sixth-form block? The study library's open.'

'Oh noooo. What if I get stuck there when people start coming in? And they see me and think I'm a serial sixth-form groupie?'

Jonah clasped my hand and pulled me forwards.

'We'll start at the other end, then,' he said, and we slipped into the first entrance to the junior high school. It was the oldest school building, made in Victorian times, with lots of long corridors and dark recesses to hide in.

'This is worse!' I whispered, as the doors closed behind us and we got used to the warmth and silence. 'Neither of us has any reason to be here.'

Jonah pushed me against the wall. 'Shhh.' He kissed me. Oh wow. And in conclusion, the point of kissing is there is nothing else on earth that feels that good. I know, whatever, there are other feelings that get good reviews. But kissing, great kissing? Accept no imitations.

We heard footsteps and Jonah pushed me again, into the dark shadow behind a wide, curling staircase. He held me there while my heart raced. A couple of Year 7 kids ran up the stairs swearing in that weird aggressive way they have of swearing, as if they think that sticks and stones are one thing but these words really can hurt people. When they'd gone, I made a move out of the stairs, but felt a sharp tug on the front of my shirt, as Jonah pulled me back. And then I was leaning against a wall again . . .

Quite a bit too much later, we emerged again, encountering a swarm of juniors who stared, but not all that suspiciously. The seniors' classrooms were in the building next door, but Jonah had further to go to the sixth-form block. I gave him a little shove in the chest, and, wordlessly, looking happy and ruffled, he went. I straightened my own shirt, and trying to keep the smile off my face, headed to registration.

Almost every day that week, I had lunch with Jonah and his mates in a greasy-spoon café a couple of streets from the school. Just like the cinema where I'd first met them, this wasn't really a school hang out, they seemed to find places that were stranger, with older people. It added to the feeling that I'd moved on to a new chapter of my life. If they minded a girl muscling in, a younger girl, too, they didn't show it. We always started off quietly and ended up very loud, making each other laugh, talking about serious things. The conversations I was having with my old friends now seemed impossibly stupid, and it sometimes made me angry: soap operas, calories, film stars' bodies. Just this endless rating of famous women – who was pretty, who was desperate, who was up her own arse. And Jonah's mates agreed with me about how pointless and destructive it was. The guys in my year would have rated the women we talked about on a different scale: whether or not they'd deign to have sex with them, with real outrage reserved for the imaginary attempts the not-hot-enough ones might make to seduce them. It felt weird talking to guys and not having to brace myself for the inevitable sexist attitudes.

But while they were expanding my horizons, they weren't making a lot of friends. They told me about the general studies lessons and the follow-up forum discussions, Sam Bond pupils breaking out into capitals, getting riled and threatening, and how weird it was that the school thought that was healthy discussion. But it didn't bother them, they thought it was funny. For instance, apparently some vicar's son had been arguing with them about people's right to believe in creationism.

'Except we are right,' Steve said, laughing. 'We *have* evidence, honest-to-goodness, hold-it-in-your-hands-and-feel-the-weight-of-it evidence.'

'Meanwhile they come back with stuff about Noah's Ark washing away all the proof and . . . uh . . . resetting radio-carbon dating, or something?' Dom said.

'They have a book,' said Steve. 'Poorly translated and hugely manipulated over several thousand years. Oh, and faith. Bollocks to faith. I'd rather get hit in the head by faith than a dinosaur bone.'

'A six-thousand-year-old dinosaur bone,' Lewis said, and they all laughed.

'This guy doesn't even believe in creationism,' Jonah said. 'He's just saying it's a good thing if people believe these fairy tales, because he says they need to believe life has meaning and that's where it gets really dangerous.'

'But why is it dangerous?' I said. I liked to ask questions. I was still weighing everything up. I honestly didn't have an opinion most of the time, I wasn't playing dumb. 'I would like to believe life had meaning.'

Jonah gave me a little smile. 'Because when people are allowed to use religion to explain history, they're allowed to use it to judge behaviour, and to enforce behaviour, and those books, those stories that someone made up, can be reread by any psychopath to say anything from abortion is always wrong, to women shouldn't be educated, to —'

'Oh, Sharia law, that's what they want,' said a workman at the next table. He had a quite high voice, and it temporarily silenced my friends and seemed to echo for a moment in the café. He seemed to wait for an answer before he tried again. 'They'd like to make us cut people's hands off and put women in tablecloths,' he said. 'I mean, the cutting people's hands off is one thing – cheaper than prisons I suppose, but women in tablecloths? Wouldn't like that much!' Then he laughed. And we laughed too, sort of pretending it was at whatever he was laughing at, but we all met each other's eyes and I had to stick my fingernails into my palms so I didn't just *howl*.

On the way back, Jonah and I fell a little behind the others, walking with our arms around each other, and we reached the school gates at the same time as Ian and Sophie.

'Oh, hi Cass,' Ian said.

'Hi,' Sophie said. One syllable, and it managed to sound silvery and breathy and feminine. I always thought I sounded like a teenage boy whose voice was just about to break.

73

'Hi,' I croaked.

Jonah squeezed my waist.

'I can't remember . . . did Issy say you were coming round to her thing tonight?' Ian said. 'I'll be passing through, obviously, so . . . might see you later?'

'Um, yeah I might be,' I said, feeling a bit helpless. Isobel hadn't asked me round to hers, although we did usually spend Friday nights watching a film there. Josette's party had been the only recent exception.

'Girls' night tonight, then?' Jonah said, as we walked in. I'd told him that Ian had been my boyfriend before him, and he'd seemed reassuringly uninterested, just a little smirk playing around his mouth when he said he knew him. A good response, I thought.

'It's just what we usually . . .'

'No, no! Only a crazy person would try to muscle in on a girls' night. I'll make sure my compadres and I get up to something appropriately manly as a response. Maybe we'll start a fight in a snooker hall.'

'Just make sure you don't get Lewis into trouble. His mum'll kill you.'

During afternoon registration, Isobel leaned back on two chair legs and sang, 'Caaass-i-deeee!'

'Iiiiii-so-belllll!' I sang back.

'My place tonight for the usual? Or are you blowing us out for a hot date?' She grinned around the pencil she was chewing. Good, so I was invited after all. In spite of the snub of Josette's party, I'd really been the one neglecting my mates this week, not spending lunch hours with them and never going out in the evening because I was trying to bank good-girl points with my mum in the hope of negotiating longer weekend nights out.

'Who is this hot date, anyway?' Dee said, joining me as we headed out of the classroom. 'Sorry you couldn't make it last week, by the way, but the film was terrible anyway.'

'No, I'm sorry,' I said. 'And I bet the film I ended up seeing was a lot worse. He's called Jonah. I'll point him out to you the next time I see him.'

'Jonah . . . he's not in our year, then? Sixth-former?'

'One of the new ones.'

'Ahh, okay.' A look of disappointment, somehow, flashed over her face, but it was gone so quickly that I wondered if I'd imagined it.

'What have you got next? Physics?'

'Yeah. Double: over an hour of Mr Hapssen's armpits. You?'

'Freeeee period!'

'They're called *study* periods?' she said sarcastically.

I cackled like a Bond villain.

Our form tutor called her over: 'Diyanah, can I talk to you before you go?'

'The day just gets better,' she whispered to me.

'We've got English later, right? I want to catch up with you.'

'Yeah, last period. And me too. We can come up with something new to make people tut at us.'

She winked.

Chapter 6

At first, it wasn't even weird. It was just me and the girls, doing magazine quizzes, watching telly rather than the movie we'd rented because every time someone tried to put the DVD in, another of us would go, 'Can I just see what happens in *'Stenders*?' or some other programme. And talking, and laughing and screaming sometimes so that Isobel's mum came in and told us to keep it down.

But then Ian came in and decided to join us. This had happened a few times since Ian and I broke up. Not to begin with, but when it became obvious that Ian and I were going to be cool with each other. Tonight, when he sat down, it was obvious that he was a bit drunk. He was louder even before he started talking: his breathing, bigger, clumsier movements, just a kind of buzz around him. He started off just talking about the programme we had on, then he suddenly said, 'Cassidy?' and everyone jumped.

'Hey, Ian,' I said, as if he'd just walked in the door.

'So what's the deal with Jonah? How long have you known him?'

'Well, about as long as you, I guess,' I said.

'How come? Where did you meet him? In school?'

'No, I, er, it was just at a café, I mean, we were both in . . .' I trailed off, because I could tell the others were finding the conversation as weird as me.

'I dunno,' Ian said. 'I probably shouldn't say anything. But I'm not sure he's a nice guy. I know there's no reason you should listen to me, and that it's weird me saying that and —'

'It *is* weird,' Isobel said. 'Shut up, Ian.'

'Yeah, sorry,' Ian said. He ran his hand over his hair. Then he sat with us in silence for another couple of minutes, while I tried to work out how I was going to ask him the right questions to follow this up. But just as I was getting them straight in my head, he'd stood up again and walked out without a word.

'Has he said something to you?' I asked Isobel.

'No,' she said.

'So . . . ?' I frowned. 'What does he mean? He must have said something.'

'He would seem to be a bit . . . jealous? Could that be it?' Finian said.

'I mean, guys, it *could* be,' Isobel said. 'But he's – no offence, Cass – properly loved up. I mean, they get on *really* well, him and Soph. Honestly, though, he hasn't said anything to me. I would have said. Well, maybe I wouldn't, but I would say now. I promise.'

'You can still be jealous even if you have a new girlfriend, can't you?' Finian said. 'You can still have feelings for someone even if you've moved on. I read somewhere that it's worse for boys than girls, in fact.'

'What does he know about Jonah, though?' Kim asked.

I could see on their faces that they were running through the possibilities. It was embarrassing and annoying, and I wanted to run after Ian and yell at him. The only possible explanation *was* jealousy, and I knew all about still having feelings for someone even when you'd fallen for someone else. Like, if they were ever yours, you still own a piece of them. But I would never let feelings like that show. Ian and Sophie had been going out for months now and I would have died rather than walk into a room full of Ian's friends and say something bitchy about Sophie.

'Shall we put the film on?' Isobel said, and everyone agreed.

On Saturday morning I had a shopping date with Sam. He'd agreed to restyle me to 'match' Jonah. His theory was that it was really important that a couple looked like a couple, like they belonged with each other, and not like they'd 'both received invitations to a party with different dress codes written on them'. But Sam and Jonah hadn't met, so Sam needed to make sure we were talking about the same person.

'Otherwise,' Sam said, 'I'm going to style you as someone else's girlfriend, and when you get around to meeting *him* sparks will fly.'

'If only things worked like that!'

'He's the black-haired white Malton boy, right?' Sam said.

'Well, there can't just be one.'

'The one I'm thinking of is very good looking.'

'I'm obviously going to agree with that.'

'Friends with a big block of blond beefcake – the aforementioned rugby player? And a weirdy beardy.'

'That's definitely him.'

'I think the trouble is, we would do better styling him to match you.'

'Aw, Sam, thank you! I think . . .'

We headed round the usual places, Sam relaxing in changing rooms while I made myself hot and sweaty squeezing into clothes that I thought would tear, tangling myself up in underslips and realising too late that there was a side zip. More than once, I caught him trying to hide a smirk.

'Okay, Sam, what's the look we're going for?'

'Ali MacGraw.'

'Who?'

'As long as I know, you don't have to worry. You can google her later.'

'Has she got curly hair?'

'No. The opposite. Very very straight.'

'Then it's never gonna happen.'

'Can't we straighten your hair?'

'You're always telling me *not* to straighten my hair.'

'And I'm right. *Never* straighten it. Okay, try these.' He handed me a pair of white trousers.

'You have to be kidding.'

'Wait till you see the full look.'

I ended up buying a drop-waisted sailor-suit dress, which might sound hideous but honestly, you'd like it. Well, maybe you wouldn't, but it suited me. Yes, Sam picked it.

As we were heading into the bus station, we ran into Dee and her older sister Afiqah. There was twenty minutes till our bus, and we waited with them in the coffee shop. Afiqah was at university, but she lived at home.

'I'm thinking of not going to university,' Sam said, biting the chocolate off a Twix.

'Why not?' Afiqah said.

'First of all, I'm not that bright, so I would have to

work really hard to get there. Then I'd have to work really hard if I got there. And what for? It's no real help in getting a job.'

'Well that's not true,' Afiqah said. 'And what about, you know, sounds corny, but the life experience? And you're not really convincing me that this is why.'

'You're right,' Sam said. 'It's not about the work, and it's not about the job. It's . . . I don't think I would like the people there.'

'There are so many kinds of people there,' Afiqah said. 'You'd like someone. There would be someone for you. I don't mean romantically. Although, you know, in terms of meeting other guys you'd be hard pressed to find anywhere as cool and understanding as university.'

'Again, I know all that is true,' Sam said. 'But there seems to be a university personality that everyone there shares, and it's sort of . . . desperately having fun.'

Afiqah laughed. 'Am I one of these desperate funsters?'

Sam paused, his lips twitched with a smile. 'You're just naturally fun,' he said.

'I'll take that,' Afiqah said. 'Listen, don't set yourself off on a path where you define yourself by this decision. You'll get used to telling people, it'll be a part of you: "Oh, I'm not going to university." You'll like saying it, you'll enjoy the response and get better at shocking them with it. And then it becomes harder every year to break free from it.'

He rubbed his hair with his hands. 'You're so smart. I can see myself doing that, actually,' he said. 'Oh, look, sorry, I didn't mean to make this a counselling session about me for me! Everyone talk about other things now!'

'Well, now my mind's gone blank,' Dee said.

'We could talk about Cassidy's hot new boyfriend,' Sam said.

Dee started to say something and then stopped very quickly, so this weird half-word came out of her mouth but she didn't correct it. She glanced at her sister, who glanced back.

'What?' I said.

'What?' she said.

'What were you going to say? And what was with the look?'

'There was no look!' Dee said.

'Oh, there was a look,' I said.

Dee pushed herself away from the table with both hands. 'Pffff,' she said.

I just waited. Sam didn't say anything.

'Your boy and his friends making names for themselves,' Dee said. 'I don't think they're good names, and I don't know how serious it is.'

I felt sick to the stomach. And in her face, I recognised Ian's expression at Isobel's house.

'Malton boys are never popular,' Sam said. 'It's a jealousy thing. And some of them are hotties, so that goes double.'

'What is it, Dee?' I said. 'What are people saying? And who's saying it?'

'There's . . .' She stopped, thought, carried on. 'There's some guys who've been saying they're racists. And quite seriously. Like they've got something to prove. I know you, and I know you wouldn't go out with a racist, and obviously if he was a racist, it would have come up, right?'

I frowned. 'This is just crazy. Of course they're not racist.'

'Look, you know them, and I don't, Cass,' Dee said.

'But why?' I said. I looked at my watch. The bus would be here soon, and Dee and Afiqah went a different way. I didn't mind missing mine if I could get to the bottom of this.

'I don't know much about it,' Dee said. 'There's some kind of online project some sixth-formers have been working on, including my brother. And there's a lot of fighting on it, they're talking about closing it down because it's too controversial or argumentative or . . . *disruptive*, or one of those things. And your boyfriend – Joe, Jonah? – is one of the ones in the middle of it all.'

'You have looked it up, then?' Afiqah said.

'Barely,' Dee said. 'After Nash told me about it, I had

84

a look. I mean arguably what they're saying isn't racist, it's against all religions. But you can't decontextualise statements.'

My head got woolly when people were using words like 'decontextualise', particularly when I was already reeling. I knew what she was talking about, they'd mentioned it a lot, laughing at how riled up the old school boys were getting.

'Religion?' I said, dumbly. They talked about religion all the time. They were very *very* anti. 'What's that got to do with racism?'

'Again, this is not my opinion, I really don't know enough,' Dee said. 'But what people – well, Nashriq and his mates – are saying is that they seem to have a particular problem with Muslims. And there are a lot of Muslims at our school who are getting pretty upset about the *way* they're talking, and, well, as far as I know it's all hitting the fan.'

I felt my skin turn red. They did talk about Muslims with me there – it seemed like a taboo-breaking way of joking, because everyone knew Muslims didn't let anyone talk about their religion. Was that a racist way of thinking? Was it even true?

'But they're not being racist,' I said. 'It's about them rejecting all organised religion. Because it starts wars, it's the reason almost everyone on the planet who's fighting is fighting. The Catholic church's line on contraception and the spread of AIDS. The oppression of women. Homophobic attacks.'

I tried to make this sound all blah blah blah, as if everyone agreed about these things, but I knew I was on shaky ground. Not because Dee and her sister were religious – as far as I knew they weren't. They didn't drink, but they'd always joined in Christmas stuff at primary school and their mum dressed like my mum, but better. The problem was that I was using borrowed arguments and if my friends had followed up on anything I would have been lost, and have had to admit it. The clever thing would have been to admit right from the start that I didn't know what I was talking about. I didn't look at Sam. Including homophobia on my bluffed list was a cheap shot that I knew wouldn't come off well.

Dee spoke carefully. 'Honestly? I would say that there is not much there that is, by itself, racist, as we understand racist. But Nash has been getting a lot more political recently.'

'Maybe it's got something to do with him arguing about this at school all the time,' Afiqah said. They shared a smile.

'So in a way, quite honestly, I think Nashriq is looking to be offended,' Dee said. 'But, in a way . . .'

'*You're* offended?' I said.

'Some of it is not good. But like I said, it's mainly

about . . .' She breathed out and began again slowly, trying to unravel a tangle of thoughts. 'The context is that we are living in a country where there is a lot of mistrust and false assumptions, especially about Muslims, and your . . . *friends* are posting links to news stories about human rights abuses in Islamic countries. But you could start listing abuse of human rights all over the world and you would never stop. And yes, there would be Islamic countries on that list, but as far as your friends are concerned that's it, stop there, forget about atrocities in non-Muslim countries. The sites they're linking to are often dodgy, and the stories are written in a way that's designed to make people look uncivilised and barbaric. And it's just like, "There, look what they're like!" But a *lot* of it.'

'You're making it sound like BNP literature,' I said.

'Look, there's our bus,' Dee said. 'Why don't you go home, read it – just search the school website, discussions, and think about it. I'm sure you know what you're doing, and you know them better than me. Maybe they don't know what they're doing, maybe if you talk to Jonah he'd be surprised there was this reaction.'

After they'd gone, Sam and I sat quietly. Sam stirred the dry foam at the bottom of his paper cup.

'That'll be our bus now,' he said.

'Sam.'

'It'll be fine,' he said. 'It's obviously a sixth-form thing. Or a Malton-Bond thing. Or a dick-measuring thing.'

'Maybe it's not him,' I said. 'When I've heard them talking, it's really Steve who's into this, the others are just giving Steve the excuse to listen to the sound of his own voice.'

'It'll be fine,' he said again, but we both stared out of the bus window on the way back, and when we reached my stop I felt almost too exhausted to walk home.

'I'm *sure* that's homework,' Paul said, in his annoying 'joke' voice, when I was clicking on the school site to find the discussion. I really didn't have time to joke about how much time I wasted on the internet.

'How about you look at the writing at the top of the window,' I said flatly, not looking up. '*Oh yes*, Samuel Bond School, my school, that would in fact make it homework, wouldn't it? And it's Saturday, and *if* I have homework I don't actually have to do it today, but it turns out I am doing. So I'm trying to work out what your problem with this is . . .' I narrowed one eye, as if really considering it.

'Terrific, you're in that kind of mood,' Paul said. 'I can't joke with you, I can't talk to you, I can only make you unfathomably angry.'

I didn't answer, just kept clicking, typing things into

search boxes. I'd found Jonah's username – everyone at school had to use the same format, their initials and then a four digit code based on their birthday and school year. And Nashriq, Dom, Steve, a lot of other sixth-form boys I didn't know. Lewis popped up now and again to supply dorky science facts against creationism.

On the whole, though, it was like Dee had said. There were dozens of links posted by Jonah, Dom and Steve to stories about oppression in the Middle East and Asia, consequences of Sharia law, honour killings, bombings of girls' schools, execution. In between these were long threads of discussion, Jonah's side getting more sarcastic as Nashriq's side got angrier. It was hard to keep a clear head when I was trying to read it. And some of the posts had been deleted by a school moderator, but the replies were left, making it obvious what had been said.

Nash: *You're free to believe all religion is 'mumbo jumbo from bongo bongo land' if you like, but it is a very simplistic view. To compare Islam to witch doctors just shows how little you understand.*

Whether an all-powerful being created Earth or whether it just randomly appeared out of absolute nothingness is something everyone needs to work out for themselves. Religion should not be used to answer questions about science and it's misleading to say all followers of religion use it for that reason. There are

89

Christians who don't believe in evolution and Christians who've furthered scientific advancement. There have been great Islamic scientists throughout history. There doesn't have to be a conflict.

You have also misrepresented 'Islamic law' as you call it (i.e. the Madhahib) but it's clear, given the level of your debate up to now, that you haven't read anything about the thing you're mocking. The simple fact is that portraying Islam as a deeply divided group of sects, all constantly fighting over minor interpretations is false. I won't pretend the Islamic community is a shining example of unity, but there are beliefs that are important to us that do unite us. NOT violent beliefs.

Steve: *Muslims are united? Presumably you all agree with the parts of the Koran that say the sun orbits the Earth, not to mention the belief that all homosexuals and adulterous women should be stoned to death.*

Nashriq's posts were angry, but clear and clever, and made sense to me. My friends' posts were more like taunts, especially Steve's, and Steve didn't listen to a word Nash said, he just kept repeating whatever he'd said. But even so . . . Jonah's links made depressing reading. If the horrible things they claimed were happening in Islamic countries were true, then wasn't it right that Jonah and his friends showed people what was really going on, what the consequences of religious beliefs were? They didn't only talk about Muslims:

there were posts about zealous Christians in America, too: creationists, polygamists, Christians who believed that American soldiers deserved to die, not because they were fighting wars and killing people, but because the US army allowed homosexuals to enlist – they went to soldiers' funerals to scream hate-filled taunts. But reading about them wouldn't make me believe that an average British vicar had the same opinions, just because they were all Christians. So why did Nashriq think my friends were attacking the whole Islamic religion, just because they were pointing out abuses in the name of Islam? And, even if that was their intention, how was it the same as racism?

I ended up reading everything, trying to find something that told me either way that things were good or bad. And I started getting why Nashriq was so angry. When Christianity came up, it was always one little group of extremists, usually deep in rural America. When it was Islam, it was always 'Muslims believe . . .' Even my friends' criticism of creationist teaching – which I'd think of as a Christian thing – seemed to blame Muslims for forcing school curriculums to be altered to suit them. Even more worryingly, there were sexist comments about girls at school who covered their hair. By Steve, the dodgiest of the group, but that didn't mean the others thought differently. I felt for Nashriq, my friend's brother, who

I'd known for years, and who slotted sincerely and persistently into the increasingly intense discussion. I felt sorry for my boyfriend, who had managed to walk into a fight. I needed someone to tell me what I thought. I needed to talk to everyone. Starting with Jonah.

Chapter 7

Saturdays were Jonah's nights with the boys. I'd been given access to the last one, but I didn't assume there was a standing invitation and I'd heard nothing from him yet about his plans. It might have been a good idea to talk to all of them together. As usual, I'd already imagined the conversation Jonah and I would have about this on my own, supplying all of his answers, remembering his shrugs and smiles and moves. In fairness to him, he was only Imaginary Jonah, but I wasn't all that happy with what he'd said.

I decided to let him come and find me. I'd always found that when the other person had to work out that you were sulking before you could even start arguing, it gave you the upper hand in an argument. But that was with Ian. Things were very different with Jonah. It was scary to admit it – maybe stupidly, with a relationship this new – but there was a lot about Jonah I didn't know. Not this stuff at school – his *boundaries*. What made him angry. How far his sense of humour would hold. How much he trusted me not to judge him. How much he liked me. All of these doubts made me think it was going to be horrible asking him. The best thing to do right now was wait.

Right now, I couldn't face anyone else. I sat upstairs in my room, not watching telly or listening to music or reading. I could hear my mum and Paul talking in the kitchen together.

Sam texted with a joke about the day's shopping. I could tell he was trying hard to avoid talking about what Dee had said. Then a text from Jonah.

Blokes have insisted on proper blokes' night. Say I'm turning girly. Missing you badly: must see you tomorrow to make up for it.

He's nice, I thought. *He's nice, and I would be able to tell if he weren't nice. This is going to be easy.*

Paul was making his way through a TV chef's recipe book, so everything he cooked was complicated and he worked hard to get compliments for it. He sat there saying things like, 'I was a bit worried about this at one stage, but I think it's turned out okay?' and 'Is it a bit too garlicky/spicy/creamy?' when the garlickyness or creaminess was what was nicest about it. It was usually nice, but I would have happily found my own dinner, even if it was instant noodles or a Mars bar, rather than sit and say, 'No, this is delicious! Thank you so much for making it!' When I didn't say that, my mum would always say: 'Paul, this is delicious, thank you so much for making it. *Isn't it, Cassidy?*' And a compliment that consists of 'yeah' is not, in my opinion, worth making, and sounds forced, to say the least.

Although both of them had a problem with me going out too much, it was obvious that me being home was a bigger problem. It was impossible for me to forget my mum reassuring Paul that I'd move out one day, and I didn't doubt that both of them would start to find life easier when that happened. Conversations were awkward and always played over a background of unspoken anger.

'How's school going this year, Cassie?' Paul said. I didn't like him calling me Cassie. It sounded like a little girl's name in his mouth, and he hadn't earned the right to trim me down. 'Do you feel as if the pressure is really on now?'

I thought there was probably a lecture lurking behind this question, or some kind of encouraging pep talk, which would be worse. I changed the subject.

'Is it fair to say you don't like Muslims, Paul?' I said. I could hear myself sounding somewhere between a total bitch and slightly unhinged.

'What kind of question is that?' my mum said.

'It's not fair at all. Or true,' Paul said at the same time. 'Yes, I'm a Christian, but I don't think I have the right to say that the faith I was brought up to believe in is more valid than other faiths.' He leaned back in his chair to look as though he was now considering the question seriously. 'Actually, I lived with two Arabs – a Saudi and an Iraqi – at university, we enjoyed discussing religion, and in fact, I'd say that it would be harder for me to understand an atheist than a Muslim.'

'Isn't the definition of having a faith, in a god, that you would *have* to believe your god was best?' I said.

Paul put down his fork. He couldn't eat and speak at the same time. When he did this, I always thought it was rude to keep stuffing food in my face while he spoke. Although part of me always wanted to be rude to Paul, another part of me obediently put the fork down, even though I wasn't even being asked to.

'If it makes you feel any better, Cassie, my god *is* the best,' he said, and winked at my mum. 'But it's polite not to tell other people that.' Then he and my mum chuckled as if this was brilliant stand-up comedy.

'Why are you talking to Paul as if he's an evangelist?' Mum said.

'Believe it or not, it's actually a school project,' Paul said. 'I had a glance at the website Cassie's been on this afternoon and there's a bunch of kids talking about exactly this.'

'Why did you "have a glance" at that website?'

Paul shrugged. 'You pointed it out to me in the first place. I clicked on history to find a web page I'd closed and then I opened it up again because the title was interesting. If you're trying to hide your browsing history, maybe you ought to furtively delete the cache every time you leave the computer.'

'Look, Cass,' my mum said. 'You're overreacting. No one is trying to spy on you.'

'I am struggling to understand why Paul —'

'Cassidy. You use my computer all day long. If Paul has work things he needs to deal with in the evenings, more often than not I tell him you're probably doing research for your homework and can he leave it a minute, when I know that what you're really doing is looking at pictures of popstars on heat.com. Oh no! I know that you've looked at heat.com, call the European Court of Human Rights! We have both been treading on eggshells around you, and I'm really sick of it. You're not easy to live with —'

'Don't I know it!' I said. 'I heard you telling Paul you can't wait to see the back of me.'

'Cassidy, that's completely untrue,' Paul said, but by this point my mum was crying. She scraped her chair back and walked out of the kitchen.

'That,' Paul said, leaning low to look me in the eye, 'was a really shitty thing to say.' He spoke quietly, but the swearing was a total shock and his voice was horrible and made me shiver all over. He moved suddenly and I jumped, bracing myself. He went after my mum. I was left staring at the half-eaten bowls of pasta, hugging my arms.

I wanted to go to my room, but that would put me close to them, close enough to hear them breathing. So I had to stay downstairs. I didn't know whether to clear away their food. What if they came back to eat it? What if they came back and said they couldn't believe I hadn't even cleared the kitchen? So I did nothing, bracing myself for the criticism. And I was furious, furiouser at being the one made to feel guilty and worried.

I wrote a text to Jonah and left it in my outbox unsent while I considered my options. I was too nervous to call him. He and his mates would be watching a film or hanging out in a pub or something, he'd be mortified if he had to take a call from his crazy weeping girlfriend. Although . . . I wasn't weeping. I was dry-eyed and cold and still angry. But I couldn't call Jonah because I barely knew him. Even with our closeness, that flame that ran underneath my skin when he touched me, that look he gave me that told me he got me, I couldn't ask him anything, I couldn't talk to him or expect anything from him. I couldn't trust him not to be horrible. He was just some guy I knew, who'd made me smile, a lot.

And then the weirdest thought came into my brain: I should go to bed with Jonah tonight. Not just to strike out at my mother for making me share a house with a man I hated – this was something I needed. I wanted to lose myself in Jonah, trust him, be so close to him that nothing could hurt that. Yes, I was angry too. It was like hundreds of men in a mine, banging on the door to be let out. I didn't want that strength, that anger inside me. I wanted someone to hold me tight and calm me, to wrap me up in their arms the way my dad had when I was a little girl. I didn't know if I'd get that feeling from him. I had no way of knowing he wouldn't turn cold the moment it was over. I had no access from this side to the Jonah on the other side, even less to my own emotions. But anyway, I called him.

Whatever happened, it was going to make a story for my children. Well, my darlings, as it happens I lost my virginity with a *racist*.

At ten o' clock Jonah and I were still walking around the streets near my house watching the strange late-night joggers. They tended to be old – white-haired, low-breasted men in sagging vests that showed all of their armpits, or tight leggings under tight nylon underpants that made them look like pensioned-off superheroes.

Jonah had been in the pub with his friends when I

called, but he left straight away, telling me not to worry. I stayed outside, walking along the same bit of pavement, the time stretching to forever, the cold and dark making everything scary, and when I saw his face I knew I was safe.

I didn't talk about the things people at school had been saying. The pressure of keeping something from him was always there, but my heart answered the same way every time: I don't even care. I'd read enough of it to know that at most the fuss was exaggerated. Everyone was jealous, the whole school, especially Ian.

'I'm fun, you know,' I said. 'Because since you met me, you'd be forgiven for imagining that I spend most of the time being all lonerish and tragic. But I'm not. You've known me a fortnight and I've been as much fun as Christmas in Albert Square, but it's just been – honestly – a weird two weeks.'

'I think you're fun,' he said, nudging me with his shoulder.

'And the mad thing is,' I said, 'this has been a great two weeks.'

'Cassidy,' Jonah said. 'You don't have to explain yourself. I'm not seeing all this angst you're angsting about. I'm not confused about who you are. You're just a very cool, very hot, non-airhead. Clever people think a lot. Thinking will get you down sometimes.'

100

'I'm not clever,' I said.

He pursed his lips, nodded. 'Yeaahh.'

I wrapped my arms more tightly around him. 'Why are you so nice to me?'

'Most people are nice,' Jonah said. 'It's not entirely selfless in my case, though.' He kissed my face. 'Okay, it's too cold. Where am I taking you now? Back to my house, or shall we just take you back home?'

'I don't want to go home.'

'But it's a good idea to go back with me,' Jonah said. 'Put them on edge. And you'll be brave with me. We'll just march in, exchange pleasantries, put some music on and snog in your room.'

We held hands as we walked in the door. Paul was on his way upstairs with two mugs of tea, I guessed that my mum was taking a bath. He looked surprised to see Jonah and, as Jonah had predicted, this unsettled him. His whispery threateningness disappeared: he was instantly nervous, being over-polite and trying to shake hands. Our house looked dark and untidy, small and overstuffed, too hot, everything carpeted and cushioned. It was so different from Jonah's house, with its high ceilings and wooden floors, where his parents laughed with Jonah's friends and gave us all wine.

'Can I make you a cup of tea?' he said. 'The kettle'll still be hot.'

'That's okay,' I said. 'We're fine, I think.'

'Okay,' Paul said. 'Well, your mother and I are having an early night. If you're watching TV, not too loud, eh?'

He seemed normal and reasonable. Maybe Jonah was wondering if I was a drama queen.

'Most parents behave around strangers,' Jonah said, when we were in the kitchen and I was looking for snacks. 'The ones you have to watch out for are the ones who make a point of keeping up the crazy act in front of your friends. I used to go out with a girl, when I was younger – about fourteen? – and she was giving her mum a bit of lip and her mum thrashed her, on the bottom, in front of me.'

'Wow.'

'It was so messed up. She wanted to infantilise her, remind her that she was a kid. Seemed to go on for ages. It was totally alien to me, that kind of power struggle, because my parents are . . .'

'Sane?'

'Far from it! They're quite accommodating, though. They don't try to put me down as a way of storing up intimidation for later. I was almost hoping Paul would ask me more questions, or at least warn me not to lay a finger on you.'

'You didn't think Paul was that bad?'

'No.'

'But you didn't think I've been making it all up?'

'It sucks, but he's probably not worse than a lot of dads.'

He's not a dad, I didn't say. I found some nuts, just so we had something to pick at if the conversation got difficult, and poured us both glasses of water. My mouth felt fuzzy and I wondered if I could go and brush my teeth. I looked around me, wondering what to do next.

'We could stay down here,' I said. 'It's further away from them. But there's no door.' I already felt like a different person with him, with everything exposed. When he didn't know anything about me, I could be cool. Now, it was all too obvious. He was different too, maybe because I was being weird, maybe because he was disappointed. 'We'd be able to hear them, I can always hear them talking in the next room, which obviously means they'd —'

'Be able to hear us, yeah. It's okay. We'll turn on some low music. They'll appreciate that as much as we will. Come on.'

He held my hand as he led me upstairs. Then at the top of the stairs he turned around to laugh. 'I have no idea where I'm going.'

I laughed too. 'There, on the end. I'm just going to use the bathroom.'

I brushed my teeth without toothpaste, so he

wouldn't know I'd done it, in case it seemed unfair, or trying too hard. My mum's and Paul's splayed toothbrushes were in the cup next to the sink. They looked vile and I wished I could hide them from Jonah. I brushed my hair, making it frizzier, then patted it down with just-wet hands. In the mirror, my reflection was pale, almost green, taking on some of the colour of the walls. And I looked scared.

Now. What was my plan?

When I went into my bedroom, Jonah was sitting on the bed, reading a magazine. I saw the room the way he might have seen it: hideous flowery bedspread, old-fashioned art posters, stills of old film actresses I liked, too many beaten-up shoes. My life looked rubbish. Jonah looked up at me through his thick hair. I didn't want to assume he still liked me.

He held out his hand and I sat down next to him. It was strange to feel so unsure of myself in my own bedroom. Gently, he lifted my hair away from my neck and kissed me. The kissing felt amazing, but my brain kept getting in the way, nagging until I lost the moment. I needed to be sure about things. Quite honestly, I'd have liked to sit and plan everything beforehand, establishing that he really liked me and didn't find parts of me physically hideous. I'd felt okay-looking walking with him outside earlier, but being here, so close and alone, changed everything.

Now I was messy and big and there was too much fleshy skin all over my body. When he touched me, I couldn't let myself feel, I was too busy trying to suck myself in and move myself out of the way. I started saying silly, mundane things, and Jonah just said, 'Shhh' and kept on kissing me, pushing me with his chest and shoulders into a flatter position. I lay back and let go and tried to relax. Sometimes I opened my eyes to peep at him, and the sight of his closed eyes was almost frightening, as if I were seeing something I shouldn't, and might get caught.

When his hand moved up from my thigh, I broke away. I'd wanted to do something tonight, to grow up and move on and make a statement. But now the time had arrived I couldn't do it.

'I have to talk to you,' I said.

'Shh, don't need to talk,' Jonah said.

'No, I do,' I said. 'I'm not all that good at this.'

'You're doing okay,' he said, through a smile, kissing the side of my neck.

'I mean, I'm . . . I haven't gone all the way.'

Now Jonah pulled back and looked at me. 'We're not going to do that,' he said, his face very serious, his voice very gentle. 'This is not how we're going to do that. I just want to hold you.'

'But I do want —'

'I just want to kiss you.'

I kissed him quickly, wanting him to feel that I trusted him. 'Am I okay?' I said, not sure why I'd said it.

'You're beautiful,' he said, understanding.

Chapter 8

It was time Sam had an opinion. I called him and asked him to meet me. I didn't even think of talking to my girl friends. There was too much to explain to them, and I couldn't tell if they wanted to hear it. They had to be talking about me. Ian must have said more to Isobel, and Isobel must have been talking to the rest of our friends. The deeper in I got with Jonah, the further away I felt from everyone else.

It was a Sunday morning. I walked past St Cecilia's church to meet Sam and saw people going inside. I had a weird urge to join them. I wondered if it could be another place to get away and become invisible, like the cinema had been, the day I met Jonah. The thing is, it wouldn't have been my first time.

My mum found out my dad had a child with another woman when I was about nine. She went mental at first, but that was when she thought she was kicking him out. Then she found out he was already leaving her. She went quiet. It was horrible. I used to walk home from school with a friend who lived a few doors down the road from me. We'd talk all the way back, but as we got closer I started to feel sick and trembly, knowing I had to go into a house that felt completely empty, but wasn't. Mum was there, pretending not to cry, making me eggs for tea every night, not talking about my dad. At night I prayed. I asked God to make it all turn out to be a mistake. When that didn't come off, I asked God to let my dad find a reason to come home. Then I asked God to make my mum go back to being the way she was. None of this happened but I didn't stop praying for it.

One sunny day my friend was off sick, but my mum didn't know about it, and I walked home on my own. It wasn't a very long way, I wasn't scared. As I was going past St Cecilia's I saw that the door was open, and I looked inside. It was empty. I looked around for a vicar, but there was nobody there. I was just a little kid, I'd never been the only person *anywhere* before. It was cool and smelled of wood and it was so lovely. I was sure I'd get told off if someone found me, but for a moment I stood just inside the door, and whispered to the statue of Jesus, asking the things I used to pray for at night. I still didn't get them, but, I dunno, I suppose

I felt that someone was listening, and it was nice.

So when Jonah's friends talked about what idiots people who believed in God were, when Steve said they had some kind of mental imbalance or personality defect, or a need to think they were better than anyone, I got nervous. Sometimes I still prayed, I still liked whispering my problems aloud and asking to be helped and feeling hopeful while I asked. I worried that something in my face would give me away. They'd think I was an idiot or a hypocrite or both. I didn't even *feel* religious, I didn't believe in the Bible or any of the things that told people they were sinful or anything like that, but I *think* I thought there was someone listening.

I noticed that Sam's hair had grown. He was looking a bit wild. We might have looked like brother and sister if my hair was darker. My 'real' brother, Nathan, my dad's other kid, didn't look anything like me.

'How come I'm seeing ten times as much of you since you got a boyfriend?' Sam said. 'Shouldn't it be the opposite?'

'Oh, don't get sick of me yet,' I said. 'I need you!'

'You haven't needed me since you gave up the band. And even then you only needed me because I always had spare reeds and you always split yours.'

Sam and I had met through the school band: we both played clarinet, and he was better than me, even though he was a year younger. I gave up when I started seeing

Ian all the time, there just didn't seem to be enough time to go to every practice and to waste a weekend a month playing charity performances in old people's homes, when I wanted to see my cute boyfriend. I loved it, but I had to leave. Maybe the trouble with me was I'd always made too many sacrifices to try to please boys.

We walked through the park and sat still on swings in the small corner playground. It was always deserted because it was tiny and falling to pieces, plus there was a fancy new one just a few streets away. The only people who used this one were teenagers, and there were often chip trays and alcopops bottles lying around it.

'Just tell me . . . what do you think about that thing with Jonah?'

'What thing?'

'You know, the arguments, if he's on the wrong side.'

'How can I tell that when I barely know him? You must have an idea, Cass.'

'I just want to know what you think.'

Sam looked away and blew his cheeks out. 'It's *not* great,' he said. He pushed himself back on his swing.

'Really,' I said. I blew my own cheeks out.

'Well, you must know that – why ask? There's definitely a feeling you get from some of their posts that the brown people are what's wrong with the world.'

'But it's not so much Jonah, is it?' I said. 'It's more the others?'

'Well yeah, maybe. And you could look at it like this: they were new kids on the block, maybe they wanted to make a splash,' Sam said.

'But . . . you of all people, don't you think more people *should* know about what goes on in the world, and what they do in other countries?'

'They?'

'Like, Muslims?'

'Why me of all people?' Sam said.

'Well . . . because you're gay and if you lived in an Islamic country that would be illegal and . . .'

'Okay, Cassidy, look, maybe we do have to talk about this.'

'That's what I want!'

'I'm a bit bothered that you came to me looking for a positive answer because you think I'd be more likely to think the same thing.'

'But that's not what I meant!' I started twisting my swing around until the chain started to knot. 'I mean, did you read some of the web pages they linked to? The treatment of gay people and women in those countries? I just thought you'd be angry about the things they believe as well.' I let go and the swing spun jerkily round, starting to spin in the other direction, then hiccupping to a stop.

Sam waited till I was facing him again. 'You have to stop saying "they", first of all,' he said. 'The things you're talking about are cultural.'

'Meaning what?' I said, impatiently, as if he was splitting hairs, but I just didn't *know* what he meant.

'I mean, it's not the religion that sets these rules, it's *some* of the people who live in a certain place,' Sam said.

'Countries, cultures, whatever, it's the same. That is what Islamic countries are like.'

'Okay, let me explain. That's wrong in about three ways,' Sam said. 'First of all, different Islamic countries have different views. Malaysia isn't anything like Sudan, or Saudi, or Pakistan or Indonesia – all Islamic countries. Second, not everyone in those countries agrees with all of the laws in those countries. There are Muslim women protesting in Saudi because they want to drive, there are gay rights in Lebanon. Those people are *all Muslims*. And third, tons of Muslims live in countries where they're not the majority and they live with the values of the countries they're in. Like here.'

'I just don't think that's true, Sam. They don't act like everyone else, they separate themselves, and I think they are judging us.'

Sam shook his head. 'Who are my friends, Cass? I've got Muslim friends. Abdul, Tareef, Rashad – Rash was in the band with us, you like him! Just ordinary geeky kids in my class who are members of the science club like me, and like *Doctor Who* like me.'

'Okay, but their parents —'

'Their parents have made kids who aren't homo-phobic, so maybe you shouldn't second-guess them. How many white kids at school do you think have a problem with me being gay?'

'Some.'

'*Most.*'

'It's not most . . .'

'Actually, a lot of the time it feels like *all* of them. White kids and black kids. Schoolkids hate gays.'

'But that's not the *law*. The law says you can't do that. Whereas in Islamic countries . . .'

Sam smiled. 'How long have we had our law?'

'I don't know.'

'Look it up. There are laws in other countries that we'd get very arsey about – even if our own laws weren't that different fifty years ago.'

'Yeah, but *now* . . .'

'Your friends are using other cultures, things we don't accept here, and trying to make us afraid of people in *this* country who follow the same religion. But not everyone who follows a religion thinks the same way, or wants to bring those laws here, no matter what Steve with the rubbish stubble says. Why aren't you talking to Dee about this?'

'Dee's not one of the religious ones.'

'Dee's a Muslim! Why don't you go out and find one of the "evil" ones, then?'

'The evil ones won't talk to me,' I said. 'They hate my freedom.'

Sam gave me a dark look.

'I'm joking! Look, what are you saying, that they're all peaceful and gay-friendly here? What about the Muslim kids at school who say they agree with what terrorists have done? Don't pretend there aren't any!'

Sam sighed. 'It's tough being a bloke. It's tough being a bloke *anyway*. And being a victim of prejudice every day, in little things people say, little casual digs, whether that's homophobia or racism or any of the things people use to make other people feel like shit, and not knowing how you slot into things.'

I had that kind of urge to laugh you get sometimes when you're embarrassed. When I used to hang around with Sam more and we went around school together with our little clarinet cases, there were comments all the time, nasty things about his 'girlfriend', jokes about AIDS, and I felt that heavy sad feeling I used to get, just from remembering it. I wanted to say something stupid to ease the moment, like, 'But you're not a gay terrorist, Sam,' but I didn't.

'It's like . . .' Sam started picking at the rust on the chain of his swing. 'If your parents are telling you to keep your head down and be like everyone else, don't cause any trouble, be invisible, but maybe you're too angry to do that. 'Cause the news is telling you Muslims' lives are worthless. It's not hard to get teenage boys pissed off and fighty: you're shown American soldiers killing tiny kids and blowing up villages, in places where you still have family, not just some vague feeling of history. Maybe people you actually know and love live there – how are you going to react?'

'But isn't that Jonah's point, that they are always going to hate us?

'But *that* stuff is not about religion. So it's crazy for Jonah to pretend that this is all British Muslims, that they're going to hate us because we're so liberal and they can't stand it. Most people who are victims of prejudice tend to understand why it's bad.'

'It doesn't have to be most, though, if there are enough people who want to kill us or change our laws.'

'Cassidy, how much of this do you believe and how much are you testing me?'

'I just wish I had some of the answers.'

'Well, why don't you ask your friends these questions? You shouldn't just nod dumbly at them saying, "Wowee, I never knew those Muslims were so dangerous."'

'How do you know all of this? How do you know you're not wrong?'

'Why are you asking me, then?'

'I'm not doubting you. I just want to know. How do you know this is right?'

Sam got off his swing and gave it an angry shove. 'It's just stuff I talk about to my friends. I'm interested because we should be interested, and I'm interested because . . . well partly it's because I'm in love with one of them. I love Rashad. He's not even gay, it's stupid. Nothing is ever going to happen.'

I got off my swing too and fought the urge to hug him. 'Love is shit, Sam,' I said.

'Yeah. Well, it doesn't have to be for you. Talk to him.'

'I will,' I said. I was so sure I would, right then. 'I just want . . . I want your permission to like him.'

'You have it.' He looked at me. He rolled his eyes, as if the serious part was over. 'You have it, Cassidy.'

'I want you to like him.'

Sam stared at me, saying nothing for a few seconds. 'Make him nice, then.'

A couple of days after that I was in a Chemistry class, copper-plating a screw, with Isobel as my lab partner.

'Do you think it'll work with my earrings?' she said. 'Let's have a go.' She snapped one into the crocodile clip and we redunked, until the big teardrop shape had a pretty little coppery bottom. 'Result! What are you doing for lunch, by the way? Are you meeting, er, Jonah? Or do you fancy coming for a panini with us?'

'Panini sounds great,' I said. There was an Italian place a few streets away that made great sandwiches, but they were quite expensive, so we tended to only have them as a treat.

'Great, I'll just text Ian and see if he wants to come.'

'Ian?' I said. 'And Sophie?' I bit my lip.

'Nah, not Soph,' Isobel said. 'Just me and my brother. Still fancy it?' She looked up – she was already texting.

'Yeah,' I shrugged.

So at lunchtime, the three of us met up to sit on a wall, holding our paninis in their waxed-paper wrapping. It was warm enough but there were grey clouds over us and I hoped it wouldn't start raining before we'd finished. Ian was teasing his little sister, and I was trying to laugh and look natural, but, honestly, I was uncomfortable. I wasn't part of their gang any more.

'How many sixth-formers are actually going to be at this Halloween bash, Ian?' Isobel said at one point. 'We know you guys are organising it, but are you just going to fleece us with big ticket prices and then leave us dancing to the *CBBC Party Album* with thirteen year olds?'

'Are you talking about that charity one?' I said. 'The Moth Ball? That's *only* for sixth-formers, isn't it? It says so on the posters.'

'There's a new thing pasted over that, now open to over-sixteens,' Isobel said. 'But all of Year 11 is assuming there's no way of checking that, really.'

'Yeah, it was just sixth form originally,' Ian said. 'And more of an excuse for a party than a charity thing. But then it looked like the tickets wouldn't pay for any kind of decent entertainment, so they opened it up to your year because they wanted to sell enough tickets to make enough to get away with calling it a charity event, then they could get local firms to sponsor bits of it. And because a lot of sixth-form guys want to perv over you and your friends.'

'That's not something my friends are going to complain about,' Isobel said. 'It's legit, then?'

'I think we're hoping it'll even be *actually* good,' Ian said. 'I'm not on the committee, but Soph is involved.'

'Are there still tickets?' I asked.

'Yeah, they want to sell loads. They've been given permission to open up the whole sixth-form block on the night, so it's a bit more creepy and house partyish, with the Halloween theme. There's teams of women at work making spiders out of old tights.'

'Oh, just women?' Isobel said, sarcastically. 'What are the "men" doing, then?'

'Don't blame me, I'm not the factory manager! I just saw a bunch of them this morning surrounded by enormous spiders and they happened to be girls. Maybe they refused to let the blokes get their hands on their tights.' Ian turned to me. 'Your lot are going, aren't they?'

'My lot?'

'I know that Steve and Dominic have bought tickets 'cause I was there when they did. Dunno about Jonah, I guess.'

'Oh.'

'You're still going out with him, though?' Ian said. He stretched with both arms, then let his hands rest on the top of his head.

Yeah, very casual, I thought, *nothing uncomfortable here.*

'Yeah,' I said. I sounded defensive. I wished that in loaded conversations like this you could practise the way you said things and choose the ones that sounded the best. I wanted my 'yeah' to sound light and innocent.

'Ian,' Isobel said, 'just say it if you're going to say it.'

'Just say what?' I asked.

'Listen, I'm heading back into school,' Isobel said. 'Come and catch me up in a minute, Cass.'

'Isobel,' I called after her. 'Well, this is weird!' I said to Ian, when she'd gone.

'It's not, don't worry. I just thought we should have a chat, face to face,' Ian said. 'You know I'm rubbish in email.'

'Yeah,' I said, smiling as I remembered the arguments we'd had when I used to interpret his emails to mean something incredibly important, and spend days being angry about them. 'But to be honest, you're just freaking me out a bit. It's that brother-sister handover, what was that?'

'I know, sorry,' Ian said. 'I just wanted to tell you, the other day when I said Jonah was dodgy, I was really out of order.' He pressed his lips together in that Ian way. 'I just wanted you to know that. It's none of my business. But we're still friends, aren't we? So I was a dick, and I think it's important that you log this one as my dickishness.'

'Oh, Ian, come on. It's fine.'

Ian pressed his lips tighter, but he wasn't smiling.

'He is nice, too, you know?' I said. 'I know all that business with him arguing with everyone earlier was a bad start as new boys, but they're just used to that kind of debating in their old school, they had debating teams. They went to inter-school debating competitions.'

'Yeah, I'm sure,' Ian said. 'Cass, you don't have to . . .' He stopped mid-sentence. I looked where he was looking and saw Steve and Lewis, then Dom and Jonah behind them.

'Well, hi, Cassidy!' Steve said, with a smile. I stood up, then stayed there awkwardly without moving forward as I wondered whether to go and kiss Jonah or something. It was excruciating.

'No, stay, it's okay,' Jonah said. 'I'll see you later, Cass.' He gave me a doubtful little half-smile and they walked on, back into school.

'Izzy shouldn't have left us,' Ian said, when they'd gone. 'Sorry if —'

'It's fine, Ian,' I said, trying to hide the impatience I felt. 'I don't need a chaperone. I'm not a Muslim!' It was supposed to be a joke about what a racist I was now that I was going out with racists. It seemed to hang there between us, so stupid and heavy and real that I felt I could grab it, but I couldn't push it away. 'That was supposed to be funny,' I said. 'And not that way. Not the bad way.'

'Yeah, I know,' Ian said. 'But there sort of is only a bad way now.'

Jonah stuck with his pack and there was no way I could get him away from them. I wouldn't normally approach him at school, so I didn't now. I was used to him coming to find me, or us both flirtily ignoring each other, throwing occasional sly glances and longing looks.

So I stood there, close enough for him to see, my eyes pleading this time. *Come and talk.* I knew he must have known I'd been talking about him with Ian because guilt shows on your face, and I knew that mine had had that guilt-filled gape when I'd spotted him. But he didn't come over now. It wasn't a total snub because we were still a fair way apart, it wasn't like anyone would have noticed him ignoring me. It was a distance we were used to playing with, though, but this wasn't playing, which meant it was fighting.

After school I tried to leave quickly and without a fuss, I didn't want to look for him and be disappointed. But he was waiting for me just outside the gate, leaning with his back to me as I walked towards him, one dark shoulder raised. He turned round to face me when I got close, as if he'd sensed I was there, or maybe it was a coincidence, or maybe he'd seen me from further back and timed it well.

'Hey,' he said softly. 'What's the story?'

'What . . . you mean . . . with . . .'

'You and your ex having lunch together and looking like you'd been caught between the sheets. That story.'

'Oh, that was mad,' I said, rolling my eyes. '*Not* my idea. I thought I was having lunch with Isobel and then Ian turned up, and then Isobel went so that Ian could talk to me alone, so I thought it was going to be some big heavy talk, and then it wasn't anything after all.'

'So, what was it?' Jonah asked. My mind went blank. I couldn't think of a lie, or how to retell what happened and make it sound like nothing, and the more seconds that ticked by without me saying something, the more my brain closed down. I can think of all kinds of lies now. Here's one: I could have said that I was having lunch with Isobel and Ian came and joined us because he's her brother and because Soph was organising the sixth-formers' Halloween party and she'd got him to try to coordinate with the Year 11s now that we were allowed to buy tickets and then Isobel had had to go back into school before us because she'd left something or had to be early for something. Okay, it's complicated, but it would have bored him out of following it up.

'He wanted to say sorry.'

'Sorry for what?'

'He got drunk a couple of weeks ago. When we were all at Isobel's. He lurched in and asked me if I knew what I was doing going out with you, or something like that, but he didn't get very far because Iso threw him out, and even before that happened all he'd said was something like . . . oh, I can't remember.'

'You can remember,' Jonah said. The tone of his voice was light and almost joky, but I knew there was no way he was going to let me get away with leaving it there.

'He literally didn't say anything bad! I think he was *going* to tell me about that, you know, like, *situation* you all got into in general studies or whatever it was, but he didn't even get around to it because Isobel told him to go away, and then he obviously thought he'd said more and couldn't remember, and wanted to tell me he shouldn't have said what he didn't even say.'

'This would all be okay if you weren't obviously trying so hard to protect him.'

I just looked at him. 'So it's not okay?' I finally said. I started walking and he stayed with me.

'He's a cock.'

'He's a nice guy. Really,' I said. 'This is more of a big deal than it needs to be.' I rubbed my eyes and face with the flat of my hand. 'Just don't . . .'

'Just don't what?'

'Just don't say anything.'

'I'm going to say something.'

'Jonah . . .'

'If he's got a problem with me, he and I should talk about it.'

'He hasn't got a problem with you.'

'I have a problem with him.'

We'd reached the top of my street. 'I have to go.'

'So go.' He stopped walking with me, but he didn't walk away, he just stood there watching me walk to my house and go inside, and it felt horrible.

Chapter 9

If you're not talking to someone it can be hard to find out if you've broken up. Jonah didn't phone or email or text. And neither did I. But I'd been the one who walked away, so I had to assume I still had a say in what happened. I wanted to call Ian to tell him there might be a problem, but it was too embarrassing. Maybe Jonah had never intended to talk to Ian. Or, while we were arguing, maybe he thought he would, but then later thought better of it. If I phoned Ian and said, 'Jonah is mad at you,' I'd be embarrassing Jonah and sending a message to Ian about the state of my relationship. I'd be doing something worse than that, too: taking sides.

I was late for school the next day, only persuading myself at the last minute that I had to go. I didn't have anyone to talk to that I knew for sure would want to talk to me. As soon as I arrived I headed for the loos and waited there till registration – because I lived so close there was only a few minutes to go. I stared at my reflection, glad there was nobody else in there. The strip lighting showed up every flaw, every hair and freckle and spot, the tiny black beetles of flaking mascara under my eyes, my dry, cracking lips. The rough, reddened skin on my cheeks and chin where Jonah's stubble scratched. I touched my lips with freezing cold fingertips, remembering the kisses and the warmth.

In registration I sat quietly and pretended to be going through my bag, my books, my pencil case, for some kind of important information. I leaned back with my legs crossed, looking like I didn't care about anything, but really I was just too shy to talk to anyone. When break came I looked for Jonah, but couldn't see him. He still hadn't tried to get in touch.

After break, I had double English, sitting next to Dee, and I relaxed – she even made me laugh. She asked if I wanted to join her for lunch, but I said I was fine before I even thought about it. I think my subconscious was too worried about her friends knowing me as that girl who went around with those Muslim-hating weirdos and what the hell did she think was she doing here? Besides, I was desperate to be alone because I had nothing to say, I wasn't interesting, and I was in a crappy mood. Also, I suppose, I was hoping Jonah and I would be working things out then.

But I didn't make it easy for him. I went out and bought a pile of junk food, which I ate walking back from the shop, then I stayed miles away from the sixth-form block. I didn't want anyone to see me lurking around it, looking for him like some idiot kid with a crush, while sixth-formers laughed and told him his stalker was outside.

It was games in the afternoon and I considered making a run for it, because no one would notice if I was standing in the corner of a football field or not. I could have taken a bus into town, gone to the pictures, found a new messed-up boy to mess me about. I stayed, though, just for the joy of being picked second to last, standing around a lot freezing, and nearly losing all feeling in one ankle when Alison Francis tackled me.

I got roped into putting some of the stuff away, and when I joined my mates in the changing rooms, I was thinking of how to explain why I'd been invisible all day, and how I'd answer casual questions about how things were going with Jonah. *That* didn't quite come up, though. Everyone stopped talking, so I knew I'd been the topic of conversation. I could have ignored this and crawled back under my stone, but I was so in the dark about everything else in my life that for once I was going to demand an explanation.

'Wow, no one's talking!' I said. I started to pull off my tracksuit, and added, 'Weird.'

'Oh, we were just discussing whether your boyfriend was a total psycho,' Finian said, casually, and a couple of girls laughed.

'What's he done *now*?' I said wearily, as if I was in on the joke. Inside, my heart was going crazy.

'Look, it's nothing. Most guys would do the same in his position,' Isobel said.

'What?' I snapped.

'He had a go at Ian at lunchtime,' Isobel said. 'According to Ian. But look, Ian asked for it, didn't he? That little private meeting he arranged with you, he must have known there was a risk you'd be seen together and he's your ex. You can hardly blame Jonah.' She smiled and shrugged at me, half-heartedly.

'I didn't know anything about this,' I said. 'What's he said?'

'Why don't you ask him?' Isobel said, and it sounded harsh, to both of us, apparently, because she added: 'I mean, Ian's pissed off about it, so he's probably not been entirely fair to him. And Ian couldn't give a crap, anyway, it's just blokes, you know.'

'I kind of expected it,' I said. 'I told him not to say anything. Is it okay? It's just blokes?'

Isobel sighed. 'Ian said Jonah was . . .' She stopped. 'What did I just say? Ian was pissed off because he did it in front of Soph, and whatever he's said about it he's not going to be fair to Jonah, so there's no point you hearing it from me.'

'But I have to hear it from you *as well*, for the same reason. Look, Isobel, you know I need to know.'

'Ian just said . . . it was pretty intense – threats, swearing, tearing his shirt.' She looked me in the eye and I was embarrassed that all of our friends were watching, but they must have known more than me already.

'Cool, though, guys fighting over you,' Finian said.

I flashed her a horrible look, but . . . had the same thought flashed across my mind? Ian was a nice guy, old-fashioned nice, never really lost his head. Jonah? God knows. I barely knew him. For every moment we'd really connected and seemed like we were meant to be together, there was another when I had no idea what he was thinking about me. I sometimes found that exciting, as if it meant he was too good for me. Did it matter what my mates thought of him when I'd been drifting away from them anyway? But maybe I hadn't been drifting, so much as being pulled.

After school I went straight to the park, sitting on the bench near the swings where I'd last been with Sam. There were some other kids from our school there, and I wondered if they knew Jonah or me.

I took my phone out of my bag and called him.

'I asked you not to talk to Ian,' I said. There was a silence.

'I talked to Ian.'

'I know.' Another silence. 'What did you say?'

'What's the point of me telling you? You can guess. He had no right. He's a . . .' he trailed off, swearing.

'But you know Ian is my friend's brother.'

'I know Ian is your ex.'

'Yeah, *ex*,' I said.

'How happy are you about that?' Jonah asked.

'I can't do this any more,' I said, and shivered. I was aware that there might be no going back, but I needed to push things forward.

'What exactly can't you do any more?'

'You know. I think we should stop seeing each other.'

'Where are you?' His voice was already slightly breathless. He was moving. In a sudden flash of paranoia I looked around myself nervously.

'I'm in the park near my house.'

'Stay there. I'll be over soon,' he said.

'It's cold. I'm not staying.'

'You have to let me talk to you.' His voice cracked, he sounded as if he was crying. 'You're not just going to finish with me without letting me talk to you. Where do you want to meet me?'

'I'll stay here,' I said.

It took him another twenty minutes or so to get there, and by the time he'd arrived I was freezing cold, blowing on my hands just to feel them. His eyes burned. He was so dark, standing in front of me like a hole someone had torn out of a picture of the park.

'Let's hear it, then,' Jonah said.

I realised I hadn't planned anything and I had nothing to say. I shrugged and looked around me. 'It's got too hard,' I said.

'I love you.'

'Do you?' I heard the words come out of my mouth, down at the end of the question instead of up, and I sounded so cold. I couldn't think of a way of undoing it. At the planning stage, if you could call it planning, it hadn't occurred to me that we would actually break up. I just needed to make a stand and have a fight, find out how I felt about him by forcing him to talk. And as soon as he'd appeared I knew how I felt. I wanted to be holding him. I wanted to get to the next stage where we were through this and okay and together like before. Now there seemed to be no way of getting there.

'Yes.' A whisper.

My heart was beating so fast that I couldn't breathe over it. 'But my friends —'

'This is just you and me. Right now, here, this is you and me and how you feel.'

131

'I don't know how I feel.'

'Okay.' He turned away from me. 'I guess I'm wasting your time.'

'How do you know how you feel?'

'You mean anyone? Or me, how do I specifically know how I feel?'

'I mean you. You specifically,' I said.

'I know because when I'm around you it's like I've taken a drug that makes me just happy. Just *happy*. When I'm not around you and I think about you, I start to buzz the same way. When I hold you, when I kiss you, it's like I'm standing in the sun and everything is great. I just can't believe it's all one way. I can't believe I'm the only one who feels the sun, that we're not both thinking the same thing. I always felt, right from the start, like you knew me and got me. That you saw the worst of me and didn't care. But if you did feel like that, you'd know. Believe me.'

But I didn't know. I hadn't known with Ian and I didn't know now. Maybe I wasn't capable of love, or that kind of certainty. The love at first sight thing, that was just getting drunk on hormones, like loving ice cream and wanting more, but not really *love*. It was about wanting them to make you feel good, not the same as caring for them like they were part of you, even when it felt horrible. Maybe if I never saw Jonah again my life would be easier. Things would go back to normal. I would see him around sometimes, but not that much. All the time I was thinking this, the movie of me and Jonah was playing in my head, the moments when it was me and him and no one else mattered, his smile, the way I felt safe when he touched me, the way I couldn't sleep at night because I couldn't wait to see him the next day. It was the same. But I couldn't tell him that.

'It's okay,' Jonah said. 'I'm not angry with you.' He smiled at me. 'I've loved being with you.' He almost laughed. 'I've had a nice time.' He was making fun of himself, sounding like a child leaving a birthday party. 'See you, Cass.'

'It's not you,' I said.

'I know, it's not me, it's you. It's okay.' Jonah started to walk away.

'It's not me! It's your friends. It's my friends.' I took a breath. 'I love you.' The words sounded stupid, as if I was a bad actress reading lines, but I meant it. I think. I couldn't get the outside me to say what the inside me felt, it was like I was trying to sabotage myself.

He turned back to me. 'Why do you care what people think?'

'Everyone does.'

'So what do you want?'

'I don't know. I know I want to be with you.'

'Do you want to go out in secret?'

I laughed. 'Yeah, a bit.'

He wasn't laughing. 'I can't do that.'

'Well, then, I suppose we'll have to just go back to the way we were. Because I can't stand the alternative.'

Jonah's face right then was the loveliest thing I'd ever seen in my life. He looked so happy, and it was for me, it was about me, and I felt happy and sorry and excited and humble.

'Come home with me?' he said.

'What am I going to tell my mum?'

'Yeah,' he nodded. 'There is that.'

'It's a school night. I shouldn't even be here now.'

'Yeah.' He reached out and pushed my hair off my face. 'I just think if I go now I'll never get you back. You'll forget how you feel and the next time we talk you'll have made your mind up. But right now I still have a chance.'

'Nothing's going to change.'

'It changes all the time. Not me. I know how I feel. But you don't really feel the way I do.'

'Why do you want that, then? That shouldn't be enough.'

'I don't think I have a choice,' Jonah said. 'I can't stand the alternative.'

It was getting dark, and I had to go home.

'Oh, there you are,' my mum said. 'Tea's ready. Listen,

would you be okay for a couple of hours? I have to drive round to a colleague and pick up a load of paperwork because she's not going to be in tomorrow and she was off sick today.'

'Where's Paul?'

'Paul's out this evening. Are you going to be okay?'

'I'm sixteen. I could be living alone at my age. I could legally move out tomorrow,' I said. I searched her face for a reaction to this. If she felt guilty it didn't show.

'I always worry about you,' she said. 'Tracey lives forty miles away, so I'll be gone till at least nine.'

'I'm fine!'

'I've made your tea. It's just ricey soup. Is that okay?'

'It's great, Mum.'

'Okay, I'll dash off now so I can be back as early as possible.'

Before she'd even got in her car, I texted Jonah: *Has your bus come yet?*

Jonah: *On it now. Why?*

Me: *Oh nothing then. Mum out for next 2 hrs ish. Alone, thought you might want to come round.*

Jonah: *Getting off bus. Only gone 2 stops. Will run.*

Chapter 10

I knew. I was looking out of the window, waiting for him, and when I saw the shape of his body, his walk with the slightly lowered left shoulder . . . I knew. I opened the door before he knocked and pulled at his arm, dragging him over the threshold.

'Are you hungry?' I said. 'My mum made soup.'

'No.'

'Me neither.'

He held my face and kissed me hard, fast, so I couldn't keep my balance, but he caught me in his other arm, and steadied me against the banister.

'You can keep me a secret if you want,' he whispered.

'No way!' I said, still kissing him. 'I only go out with you because you're easy on the eye. What's the point of a secret trophy boyfriend?'

We snogged in the hallway for a while and I was so excited and nervous I wanted to giggle. I led him upstairs and we sat on my bed and then everything seemed to slow down and I wasn't sure what was going on. My stomach rumbled and I was embarrassed.

'Maybe you should eat something,' Jonah said.

'I'm not hungry. Well, obviously parts of me would disagree with that, but I really don't feel like eating.' I leaned forwards and started kissing him again. 'I think we should . . . right now . . . I think I want to go all the way,' I whispered.

'Cassidy,' Jonah said. 'We should talk about this first . . .'

'I want to,' I said. 'I know what I'm doing.'

'But your mum will be back.'

'Not for ages.'

'But if it happens, when it happens, I want to . . . you know, hold you. All night. I don't want you throwing me out the door with my trousers over one arm.'

'Oh,' I said. I was suddenly mortified, as if he was calling me easy.

'Don't look like that. Do you think I don't want this more than anything in my whole life? I'm just not used to you being so . . . direct, it's a bit . . .'

'It's putting you off?'

'No, of course not. I just want things to be, you know, I don't want you to feel —'

'This is all the time we ever have. I can't stay with you, you can't stay with me. This is . . . seriously, have I freaked you out? I don't know how to do this. I don't know what to say. You know I *don't* know what I'm doing, don't you? I've never . . .'

I looked for reassurance and couldn't find it. I'd killed the mood. Why hadn't I stopped myself from talking? In the movies people didn't talk, they didn't try to arrange things like an over-eager puppy. They let the boy take the lead, or knew how to take the lead themselves.

'This is my first time, too,' Jonah said. He swallowed quite noisily, and I tried not to look as though I was bothered. In actual fact I was glad. It was nice, and I was relieved, but it terrified me too.

'How?' I said.

'Well . . . it just is. My last girlfriend didn't feel ready.' He looked a little like Ian as he pressed his lips together shyly.

'Oh.'

Jonah laughed. 'Don't look like that. I have a fairly good idea of what I'm doing. It's going to be okay.'

It wasn't okay. As soon as he started it hurt so much I wanted to cry. I thought I might be able to hold on, but I had to tell him to stop. I thought there must be something wrong with my body. Then I whispered that I was ready to try again, but I realised he was getting further away from me, in every sense, until he shook his head and rolled on to his back, lying with one arm on the pillow, looking at the ceiling.

I lay next to him, shrinking as much as I could in my skinny little bed, staring at the posters on my walls. When my skin moved against his, I felt like I was bothering him and he probably couldn't stand to be near me. I would have given anything to undo what had just happened. Maybe he was the right boy, but it hadn't been the right time: I didn't know him well enough. I couldn't tell what he was thinking. I couldn't laugh with him about things going wrong. I listened to him breathing and tried to make my breathing silent. If he'd gone another second without speaking I would have screamed.

'Are you okay?' he asked.

'Yeah, of course,' I said.

'Your mum's probably gonna be back pretty soon?' Jonah said, and I realised he wanted an excuse to get dressed, and to get out. I didn't want to be undressed any more either, but the clothes I'd taken off seemed too much a part of what had happened. They lay baggily all over my bedroom. I thought about my mum and felt sad, as if I'd lost some jewellery she'd given to me. Eugh, that sounds so naff! I don't mean my virginity was like a jewel, or precious, I mean, it felt as though I'd lost something that mattered to someone else too. I wasn't sure I even *had*: I didn't feel like a virgin any more, but I definitely didn't feel like I wasn't, either. I was desperate to talk about it, I wanted Jonah to say everything was fine, but he didn't.

'Yeah, I guess,' I said.

'Don't think she's going to want to find me here.'

'I'm really sorry.'

'Don't be sorry,' he said, avoiding looking at me.

I reached for my bra and put it on; it felt cold on my skin. Jonah threw on his T-shirt, putting both arms in before his head, the way boys do.

'I'm sorry, I'm really rubbish,' I said. 'I was expecting it to —'

'Really, look, don't be sorry,' Jonah said. 'Stop saying you're sorry. I should go.'

We kissed a little bit behind my closed front door, and when I opened it to let him out, he hooked my fingertips in his and gave me a sad little smile. I closed the door and watched him walking away, a reverse repeat of the moment when I saw him walking towards the house earlier in the evening, and I'd believed I could do anything.

When he'd gone I ran the bath and cried in it, adding more hot water until my skin turned pink. I'd messed up the most important moment of my life.

I was already out of the bath when my mum finally

came home, carrying a huge pile of papers in a cardboard box. She dumped them on to the kitchen table and looked around.

'Didn't you have any soup?' she asked me.

'Yeah, I did, it was nice,' I said.

'Really, and you washed your bowl and spoon and put them back in the cupboard?' she said. But she smiled.

'I just ate some junk while I was on the internet,' I said. 'I'll eat it tomorrow.'

'It's okay,' she said. 'I'm not telling you off. I never said I was a good cook. Fortunately, we have Paul.' My face must have fallen, because she stopped smiling. 'I know . . .' She sighed. 'I know you . . .' Stopped again. 'I know you don't . . . *like* Paul,' she said. She looked up at me, and her nervousness freaked me out.

'It's not about me not liking him . . .'

'And it kills me. I'm sorry, I'm not trying to make you feel guilty. If I let myself think about this, though, it is like someone has taken away all my breath and my stomach hurts and my heart hurts and I hate myself for making my little girl sad and I don't know how I can go on being selfish.'

'Mum . . .'

'I think I just keep believing you'll see him the way I do sooner or later. Because he is a good man, Cass, and he's so good for me.'

141

This just got me angry again, because at the heart of it, it was all about her and her feelings, and wanting me to agree with them, rather than her trying to see things my way.

'Well, it's not like I'm going to live here for ever, is it?' I said, trying to make her feel guilty, but also, I think, trying to hurt her. I did believe that she loved me, and that having to think about losing me would make her sad, even if she wanted it sometimes. I felt wild and reckless, mainly because I was mad at myself for being stupid earlier and wanted to take it out on someone else. But also because I'd needed this conversation and imagined having it for so long that I almost had a script to work from, as long as my mum said everything she was supposed to say.

'That's what I keep telling myself,' my mum said. 'But I'm going to have to deal with that, and I'm going to have to be grown up about it.'

I didn't really know what she meant. There was a strange atmosphere between us, I had a kind of ache through my body because she wasn't holding me, and I needed her to hold me. I kept imagining the feeling, the softening through my muscles, but I couldn't go to her and couldn't trust myself not to push her away if she tried to touch me – I felt prickly and sore-skinned. In a way, it was enough that she was there, and not telling me off. Her timing was so good I worried my face was giving something away. I had a million questions in my head, all shouting for attention at the same time, until I realised I wasn't going to ask any of them.

'It's not that I don't like Paul, Mum,' I said. 'But I don't really know him, and he talks to me as if we go all the way back. It's hard to know how to take it. I don't think I'm ever going to feel like I can talk to him like that.' I could hear the way I sounded, cold and bored-sounding, and suddenly realised it wasn't an affectation.

I *didn't* really care about Paul.

This wasn't about Paul being there, it was about my mum *not* being there. It made me so angry. I felt like she'd abandoned me without any warning, she'd just gone. Once, post-Dad, it had been the two of us, and we had been strong and amazing and loving. And all of that had ended almost in a flash, and Mum didn't even seem to have noticed, or feel like she owed me anything, and maybe she didn't. But we'd had it, it had been real, and now it was gone. Tiny little things that added up: the way she used to surprise me with little presents when she came back from shopping or baked me brownies. Not the *things*, even, the fact that I was on her mind. The way she used to come in at night and talk to me in my room until I started to drift off, the sound of her voice making me safe – even watching telly together, that almost never happened now. Gone.

And I missed it and I needed it more than ever, especially tonight. I didn't know if it was fair to resent her, because maybe she did deserve her own life back already, and she probably thought she could have both. I tried to stay angry, but feeling guilty kept getting in the way.

And then she said: 'You've already left me, haven't you, Cass?'

'What?'

'I mean, you're talking about leaving home, but you've checked out already.' She looked so sad. I hated the way she let me see her sadness. It was frustrating because I knew *I* could be exactly the same way with her and let her know how bad I was feeling, but I kept so much hidden. So many times when I'd been hurt and lonely and hated Paul and even hated her, I went to my room and stayed quiet or poured things out to an anonymous talkboard, somewhere she'd never see it. She had no idea how much I felt. Like now, I so wanted to talk to her about love – and sex – as I knew so many of my friends did with their mums – but there was no way it was going to happen, she would have freaked out. She wanted me to be a grown-up when she talked about her relationships, she always said she thought I'd want to know the truth about what happened between her and my dad – as if by being honest she was doing me a favour – but there was no way she'd have been able to take me being the same way back.

I didn't have the energy to contradict what she'd said, but she was wrong. This evening I wasn't ready to look after myself, I wanted my mum to be my mum, however she wanted to be. I walked around the kitchen table to her and put one arm around her. The whole time I was terrified she'd reject me, and she almost did, staying stiff and cool for a long time, but it was too late, I couldn't stop now. Then I felt her arms around my shoulders and smelled that Mum smell that no one else smelled like, and I stayed very still, hoping she wouldn't let me go.

Chapter 11

The next morning, I ran into Dee outside the school gates. She seemed to have been waiting for me, and looked stressed out.

'What is it?' I asked.

'You're not going to like this,' she said. 'Well I *hope* you're not going to like this.' Her voice was tight and angry.

'What?'

'You know Nash's friend Saira?'

'I think so? Sixth-former, kind of big . . .'

'Kind of big, yes. Very fat, but so what?' She almost shouted this.

'I was just checking we were talking about the same person. Come on, Dee, how long have you known me and I'm suddenly a bitchy fat-fascist?'

'I know, I know,' she said, over a sigh. 'I'm just

worried about you.'

'Why are you worried about me?'

'Okay, so last week there was more of this stupid contemporary society or whatever it's called discussion in Nash's general studies class, and this time apparently Saira was defending the fact that she wears the hijab.'

'Oh. What did they say?' I said. I felt a sense of dread.

'Nothing *there*. But she was seeing a film with some friends on Sunday, ran into your friends, and they were pissed, and Steve was like, "Thank God you've covered up your *beauty* or we'd be completely unable to stop ourselves from ravishing you!" and he came up to her and touched her.'

'What do you mean, "touched her"?'

'Look, no big deal, I don't mean touched her up. Just put his arm around her waist. But it was horrible for her. She knows they're taking the piss because she's not pretty, and she's the one who used the word "beauty" in the class, because that's the line on the hijab, but to have to deal with pissed-up boys in the street – and she's not great with boys, she was really scared – that kind of talk is frightening and threatening even if you're not "pretty", you know!' She was furious now, talking faster than I'd ever heard her talk.

'I didn't say it, Dee!'

'Saira said there was a girl with them.'

147

'Jesus Christ, you think it was me? Saira knows me, doesn't she?'

'She wasn't sure. The girl had curly hair.'

'IT WASN'T ME!'

'Well, is there a difference?'

'What the hell? Is there a difference between all girls with curly hair? What?'

'NO!' Dee sighed. 'I'm sorry, Cass. I just mean, what's the difference between being the girl with them on Sunday night and being the girl with them tomorrow night?'

'You can't think that about me.'

'No,' she said, and she was nice, reassuring, pushing me to take her word. But I realised I was trembling.

'Was Jonah there?' I asked.

'I don't know.'

'Did you ask?'

'She said Steve and some mates and some girl. I can find out.'

'You don't have to. *I* can find out.'

'Just find out everything. Be aware of what you're into, and who you're involved with, and know that people are talking.'

'They're not racists, Dee.'

'What is it, then?'

'It's bullshit, isn't it! It's some kind of stupid showing off about how clever they are. They're just

148

parroting some books they've read.'

'Well look, Cass,' Dee said. 'Ask yourself this: is it nice?'

'No,' I said. 'It's not nice.' She didn't say anything. 'Is Saira going to tell someone at school?'

'I doubt it. It's not like she's not used to hearing crap like that, worse, in the street. She only told Nash last night, and she told him because Nash hates them.'

'Really, Nash hates them?'

'What do you think?'

'Is someone going to complain about them?' I said.

'Why do you keep asking that? Are you more worried about them being slapped down by the school than the fact that they're doing it?'

'I've got to go,' I said. 'There's no point us talking about this any more. You know how I feel.'

'Cassidy, I *don't*,' Dee said.

I walked off. Not out of anger, I just couldn't face her anymore, I was too depressed, I couldn't make myself talk.

I had to walk past the sixth-form block anyway, and I stopped outside it, looking up at the common-room window to see if I could see Jonah, but the windows were full of ads for the Moth Ball. I'd heard girls in my class discussing their costumes, some were going for those stupid sexy cat or slutty she-devil things, and in happier moments I'd been daydreaming about mine –

149

something creepy and not so obvious. I'd been waiting for Jonah to ask me to come with him, but I guess I'd been giving him other things to think about. Now, if he asked, there was absolutely no way I would go.

'Well, Miss O'Neill! Are you checking up on your husband?' It was Steve, on his way into the block. 'Would you like me to send him out to you?' His eyes flicked from my face all the way up and down my body as if he was checking me out. I thought about him grabbing Saira, and how getting attention from the wrong boy can make you feel sick to your stomach.

I was about to bleat something apologetic and run away. I remember avoiding looking at him, feeling small and flimsy. But then I forced myself to face him and saw his broad, not-quite-bearded face with that mocking, yellow, smoker's grin and I knew I wasn't scared of him, just *furious*. I had the urge to slap him and keep slapping him, could picture his cheek reddening with repeated slaps from the hardest part of my hand. I couldn't remember ever being so angry.

'You're pathetic,' I said.

'I'm pathetic?' he said. I knew that people repeated things to buy themselves time when they didn't know what to do, but his loud voice and laugh still made me wobble a bit. The fear was back, edging in on the anger, as I realised I didn't have a plan.

'I heard about what you said to Saira,' I said. 'Who do you think you are?'

'You weren't there, you don't know what you're talking about,' Steve said. 'And I've seen you laughing well enough when Joe's made jokes like that.'

'Never,' I said, biting my lip hard to stress the word. 'Was Joe . . . nah there?'

'Don't you know?' Steve asked. His grin broadened, then he frowned in mock concern. 'It seems to me you have some communication problems.' Sensing an audience gathering around us – a couple of sixth-formers had stopped to listen – he added a more obvious insult: 'Seems to me you've got problems full stop. I don't have time for this.'

'Was he there?' I asked again, even though I knew it was stupid.

'Ask him,' Steve said and the door swung shut behind him.

One crappy year's difference in our ages, but I was the loser in school uniform standing outside in the cold, while Steve was the grown-up in a tweed coat closing the door in my face and going inside to laugh with the handful of friends he still had. It was nearly registration and I couldn't wait any longer.

I was halfway back to the senior block when I heard Jonah behind me, running to catch up.

'Cassie, wait.'

I sighed, and it hurt to breathe. 'I can't, I have to go.'

'But we need to talk. Can't you be late?'

'No! We'll talk at break.'

'Yeah.' He held out his hand to take mine, but I was gripping the strap of my bag and flinched away from him.

He seemed different when we met up again a couple of hours later. Stronger, as though he'd used the time to prepare and had come back with a great case. We stood behind the gym, we didn't have enough time to find anywhere more private. Some gymnastics fanatic kid was inside flipping around on parallel bars, and when we weren't looking at each other – most of the time, in my case – we stared through the big windows at him. It was a strange backdrop, but I was glad of something to watch when the conversation was sticky.

'From what I can make out,' Jonah said, 'Steve and Dom and Dom's little brother and his girlfriend got into some kind of —'

'From what I heard —'

'Let me just . . .' Jonah said, trailing off as if it was too much for him. 'Let me just tell you how I heard it, then you tell me.'

'Fine,' I said, coldly. 'But we don't have much time.'

Telling people to hurry up with telling you something always slows them down.

'Steve and Dom and Dom's little brother —'

'Were you there?'

'No. Is that okay?'

'It's not,' I said, 'okay enough.'

'It would have been better if I'd been there?'

'It would have been easier if you'd been there. I wouldn't be listening to whatever you've got to say next. But it's not great even that you weren't there, because —'

'What, it's lose either way?' Jonah shouted. 'If I was there, if I wasn't there, it seems to piss you off just as much.'

'BECAUSE,' I went on, 'you are going to bloody defend them and this time I know for sure they are not worth defending.'

'Were *you* there?' Jonah asked.

'You know I wasn't.'

'I don't know anything about this!'

'So why are you defending them?'

'I haven't said I am!'

'We can't do this now,' I said.

'I know. When?'

'Well, lunch?'

'This is stupid,' Jonah said. 'All these summit meetings where you tear strips off me. I understand that you've had a few problems with my friends fitting into your school, and that for some reason your friends have taken against us and this is a big deal to you. I mean, I know why it's a big deal, not why your friends all hate me. But at some point, you have to ask yourself whether you need your friends to approve of who you're going out with. And at some point you actually need to ask yourself whether you think I'm a total prick or not. And if you can't honestly answer that, then maybe it's best that we don't go out at all. So look, we're not going to meet at lunchtime, you're just going to have to take my word that I am not a BNP supporter or someone who beats up women and old ladies in the street or kicks kittens in the face. And if you do take my word for it, you're going to have to come and find me and tell me, and make me believe you. Because I *literally* can't be arsed with this any more.'

'What are you saying, then? You're finishing with me?'

He didn't say anything, he seemed to be waiting for me to say something else. Then he sighed. 'Looks like it, doesn't it?'

I shut my eyes as he walked away from me. When I opened them again, the kid in the gym was throwing himself over the metal bars, his arms trembling with the tension. He stopped and looked straight at me.

'Are you okay?' Isobel asked, when we were heading into French together. I wasn't crying, I was just feeling dazed, and was surprised that something showed on my face. Maybe she'd seen us talking and looking serious, or seen Jonah walking away.

'We broke up,' I said, sitting down and taking books out of my bag. I lined my pens up carefully on the desk, as if it was important that they were exactly the same distance apart.

'Oh, why?' Isobel said, not sounding all that sympathetic. She leaned down to my desk, lowering her voice almost to a whisper. 'Well, look, maybe I heard something about some of it from Ian already. Maybe you don't want to go into it. I don't know him, but I think you did the right thing.'

'Actually, he broke up with me,' I said. This was true, but not all of what had happened. I just wanted Isobel to consider the fact that I might be shocked and hurt, because I was both. If I'd been the one to end things, she would have just thought I was angry.

'Oh,' Isobel said. She threw her bag and coat on the chair next to Finian behind me, but leaned back to me again. 'If you want to talk about it . . . we could go for a panini at lunch, or call me this evening?'

I did want to talk about it, but I had someone else in mind. Still, now that I'd told Isobel, I didn't have to tell anyone else in my year.

At lunchtime I was getting panicky because I couldn't find Sam anywhere, and then I remembered it was school band practice today, so he'd have brought in his clarinet. I found him changing a broken reed in one of the little music rooms. It was the perfect place to talk, as long as he kept putting out the odd tune to prove the room was occupied. We sat down on the carpet together.

'I wish you were still in the band,' he said. 'Clarinets have got sexist since you left. They spend too much of the time making lewd remarks about flutes and oboes and I don't feel equipped to join in.'

'Have you heard the news?' I said. 'Jonah dumped me.'

'Why?'

'I *think* it was because I kept breaking things off or nearly breaking things off and we were always in this are-we-broken-up? state.'

'That's not enough to put a bloke off. On the contrary, some of us live for that state.'

'The other thing he seemed angriest about was that, underneath it all, I didn't trust him to be a nice guy in the face of the gossip and accusations.' When I said it out loud I knew that it was true, I didn't trust him at all. It made me feel horrible, not because I should have believed in him, but because I knew part of me didn't care whether he'd been a racist or not. I would have forgiven him anything. If he'd said what I needed to hear – and before you ask, no, I don't know what that might have been – I wouldn't have cared if he'd been part of Steve's gang that night, or what he thought about Islam or any of it. I just wouldn't.

'You can see his point,' Sam said. 'Why were you going out with him if you didn't trust him?'

Because I wasn't a nice enough person to care about it? 'You're on his side.'

'Obviously not. If there *are* sides, I would punch him for you. Or speak to him harshly, anyway. I just want to understand the difference between the Jonah you thought was a dreamy boyfriend —'

'Don't make fun of me,' I said limply.

'I'm not. Really. I need to know the difference between that Jonah, and the one where you're willing to believe the worst of him. What does he do that makes it worth it?'

'He feels like my first *real boy*. Ian has always been around, he was just part of the phenomenon where everyone in our school eventually goes out with everyone else in our school. Jonah was the first person who made me feel that there might be someone in the world who thought *I* was worth it. He listens to me, he seems *excited* if I agree with him, as if I'm someone you'd want to be agreed with by! That feels nicer than you can imagine.'

'No, I can imagine.'

'And it was like, by not knowing anything about me, he was better at getting the *real* me. The me I'd always hoped was real.'

'So for you it was all about him understanding you, whether or not you felt you knew him?' Sam asked.

I wondered if he meant this was bad. 'If someone really knows you, it's like they signed up to you with full knowledge of what they were getting. So they won't ever be disappointed.'

'That can't be true,' Sam said. 'People don't get divorced after ten years because they suddenly realise what the person is like.'

'What about my mum? She found out her husband had a kid with another woman!'

'Fair point.' He stood up on his knees and started playing 'Maria' from *West Side Story*. His eyes smiled at me over his tightened lips. He finished off with a couple of scales, then he stopped and sat down with me again. 'Someone walked past. Look, Cass, I'm not going to persuade you of anything, but I've known you for a few years, and I keep finding you more adorable.'

It was one of those times I really wished I could have given him a hug.

'Anything happening with that boy you're in love with? Rashad?'

'Absolutely nothing whatsoever. No awkwardness, no arguments, no excuses, none of the things that are giving you so much grief right now. The perfect relationship.'

'But none of the nice things either,' I said.

'It's so much better this way,' Sam said. He pushed my shoulder gently with his shoulder, and the contact was so unexpected I jumped. 'You're going to love it.'

'Oh God, I don't have a boyfriend!' I said, mock-wailing. We both laughed.

'Are you okay, though?' Sam said gently.

'I am now. I may not be when I get home.'

'And when you're not, give me a ring.'

Chapter 12

My girl friends were being carefully tactful around me, emailing me funny YouTube sitcom clips about break-ups, stopping to chat after school, just talking a lot more – so I found *myself* talking a lot more. The difference was so noticeable and sudden it made me wonder how many people had actually not been talking to me when I was going out with Jonah. Maybe I'd just been charging around not needing anyone, swept up in my world with him.

Most conversations were about the Moth Ball. Everyone I knew had tickets, even the fifteen-year-olds. They knew there'd be teachers there, I suppose they just thought they'd brazen it out or wear enough Halloween make-up to be unrecognisable. The issue was clear cut for me: I was sixteen already, and I definitely *wasn't* going.

On Friday morning, Isobel asked me a couple of times if I'd come to her house for a pizza that evening. I said no first, and then I said really no, and after you've said no twice it's quite hard to say yes. I thought there was no way of going without making an entrance when I arrived, because my story was possibly the best gossip of the week. But I didn't want to spend Friday night with my mum and Paul either. So I just came out and asked Isobel, on the way out of school.

'Tonight: is the offer still open?' I asked, and I'm not sure why, but I was bracing myself, even though she wasn't likely to laugh in my face.

'Oh, yeah of course!' Isobel said. 'Okay, I'll see you tonight, then! Fantastic that you can make it! Bring chocolate!' We started walking in opposite directions, and then I heard Isobel call, 'By the way, Josette'll be there.'

Josette was just a reminder that life hadn't gone quite back to pre-Jonah normal, and it was cool of Isobel to give me the warning – not because I had a problem with Josette, just because she understood me and knew it made a difference. I would be among friends, but I might not be relaxed enough to talk – on the other hand, the evening wouldn't be all about me, now, which was good.

I turned up a little bit early because I wanted to be the first there. Isobel and I sat in the kitchen with her mum and dad while they ate their dinner, and they let us drink some of their wine. Isobel's mum asked about my mum, and Isobel's dad told boring stories about the time he worked for my mum's company. Even though I hated the taste of wine, I sipped it a lot because I had nothing to say, and I hadn't eaten anything since breakfast so I was light-headed by the time the other girls had turned up. We all crowded around Isobel's computer, looking up boys from school through their Facebook pages, leaving comments on their photographs. I felt slightly outside of my body, not really joining in the laughter, or the apparent bump in excitement of talking to someone we could talk to any day of the week in real life, just because it was through the internet. I thought about Jonah all the time, whether he'd be embarrassed by the way I was acting and the crowd I was with – which was a bit crazy given that we broke up over whether I was ashamed of him. I missed him, even though I might still have been there even if we hadn't broken up. And I missed the person I'd been with him.

But I was a bit interesting to other people now, I had a break-up story to tell, and my friends did want to hear it.

'I heard he broke up with you?' Finian said, and Isobel blushed, because who else could she have heard it from?

'It's not a big secret,' I said, to get Isobel off the hook. 'I think he thought I was messing him around a bit.'

'Did you . . . did he want to go further than you?' Finian asked.

'No, it was nothing to do with that,' I said.

'How far did you go?' asked Finian.

A smile broke out on my face without me meaning it to. 'I'm not sure,' I said.

'How come?' Josette said, and I turned to look at her face for a moment. I realised how much I'd needed female friends around me. All the attention from guys and blokey talk had been great fun and very flattering, but guys didn't talk the same way as us. I knew this was the wrong thing to do . . . but I started telling them the story of our unsuccessful attempt to go all the way. I needed to tell someone. Maybe telling *everyone* wasn't smart, but at the time I really wanted to. Their reactions were great, I got seduced by the way it seemed to make them accept me back into the inner circle, the way that sharing a secret with other people can make them trust you.

I think Isobel must have told Ian I'd be there that evening, because he didn't come in to chat with us, probably hoping to avoid a repeat of the last time when he'd been drunk and started dissing Jonah. I didn't know he was home until I went to the loo and ran into Sophie,

Ian's too-good-to-be-true girlfriend, who was coming out. *Ooh, go to the loo, do you?* I thought childishly. We both said 'hi' shyly at the same time. When I went back into Isobel's bedroom, I suddenly realised I was sad. My energy was gone and I couldn't talk or pretend to laugh any more. It wasn't the fact that Sophie was Ian's girlfriend, it was that she was *anyone's* girlfriend. She was here with a boy who was crazy about her. She would have rushed in to tell him about bumping into his ex, and they'd giggle over how embarrassing it had been (not nastily) and talk in whispers.

That's what it's all about, having a boyfriend. I know it doesn't sound exciting or romantic, but those moments when you and your pal come through awkward or embarrassing or scary things together and find them funny because you're together, he's on your *team*. All the things you do together bond you more . . . for as long as you're in love. They become private jokes that you tell each other again and again, knowing that only you two know the story of you and him.

I didn't have anyone on my team now, and I know this is nuts, but it felt like Sophie had somehow taken both of my boyfriends – first Ian, fair and square, then by being the girlfriend of the boy who was making trouble for my new boyfriend, she was guilty by association.

Back in Isobel's bedroom, the conversation had moved on to – what else – the Moth Ball.

'You're *definitely* allowed to go,' Finian was telling Josette. 'There's nothing on the tickets about the school you go to.'

'I'm not sure if that's true,' Kim said. 'What if a million people turned up?'

'Well, they know how many tickets they're selling, duh,' Finian said. 'They won't go over capacity, and it's for charity so they want to sell them all. Are you still not going?' she asked me.

'Of course I'm not going!' I said.

'Why not, though?' Finian said. 'Weren't you going with Jonah?'

'We didn't even talk about it. I think, you know, Jonah can't be doing with the rest of the sixth form.'

'To be honest,' Finian said, 'from what I've heard over that religion stuff, I think they were in the right, and actually, I think they're fantastic. I'm sorry, Cass, because you don't want to hear that when he's just dumped you, and I'm sorry, Isobel, because I know Ian thinks it was wrong, but what did they actually say that was wrong?'

'What, apart from saying that no one had a right to be a Muslim?' Isobel said.

'What they said was that no one should be *any* religion,' I said. 'And I was there, talking to them about it, so I know that's how they feel.'

'Why, though?' Isobel said. 'My parents are Catholics.

I would probably say I still am. What harm is it doing?'

'It happens to still be responsible for most terrorism, war, civil war . . .' Finian said.

'Like in Northern Ireland,' I said.

'So all wars are about religion? Do you honestly think that's what the entire situation in the Middle East right now is about?' Isobel said, with the kind of impatience that was designed to let us know she understood more than us. I didn't look at Finian because I didn't want her to see that I didn't know anything. 'And anyway, that's not the point with *your friends*. You must have heard how they seemed to have it in for Islam.'

'I'm not getting into this,' Finian said, 'but it seems to me Muslims make trouble for themselves by not fitting in, so people think they are rejecting our culture because they hate us. I'm not saying that's true, but that's what people think. When they dress weirdly, they're inviting people – maybe bad people, maybe racists, whatever – but they are encouraging people to *be* racist, because they look weird or scary.'

'So they're saying we should ban nuns, then?' Josette asked. 'Let's rip the big dresses and funny hats off those poor, oppressed white women?'

'Yes they are, though!' I said. 'That's the whole point. And I'm not aware of us having any nuns in our school.'

'How about goths? They look weird and scary and

people beat them up for the way they look too,' Isobel said. 'Should we draw up the way people have to dress in parliament?'

'So you're okay with *only* women walking around totally covered up because guys apparently can't control themselves so no one would blame them for raping us if we flaunt our sexy noses?' I said, nearly shouting.

Isobel was also really loud. 'I'm not talking about a burqa, I'm talking about any outward sign that you follow a certain religion, which seems to be what they have a problem with. Why shouldn't someone be allowed to cover their hair? From what I heard, in Steveworld that would be outlawed.'

'Oh, you're just parroting what Ian tells you,' I said, but I hadn't known that everyone knew what Dee had told me about her brother's friend Saira. It was horrible to be publicly associated with Steve, to be seen by people I knew as thinking like him, when in reality I couldn't bear him now. And I didn't want Finian to be on my side, either, because Finian was kind of an idiot. Frankly, I didn't much want *me* to be on my side. It was Jonah's side, and he was my ex who I was going to get over when I got round to it. And yet, that was where I found myself, angrily arguing something I had never cared about, because of him.

This wasn't how break-ups were supposed to go. The boy was supposed to find someone else. Or you were. Or something, but at least one of you was supposed to hate the other at some point.

I had a weird dream that night. I dreamed that I was going out with Ian and he was breaking up with me all over again and I was crying and trying to reason with him. Then we were kissing and kissing and it was wonderful, but when I woke up I realised that all through the dream the person I'd been calling Ian and thinking was Ian was Jonah, with Jonah's face and voice, and even the way Jonah kissed. And I missed him so much. *Jonah.*

Pizza night at Isobel's had made me realise there was nothing about my old life that I'd been missing as much as him. The girl talk had been lovely and warm and comforting, and then it had turned quickly, as girl talk often does, to something more like a competition. Call me a guy's girl, but that didn't really compare to girl-boy things: warm hugs on cold days, secret kisses, feeling like the romantic lead in a movie rather than the lonely, sarcastic best friend. It would be simple to go back to school on Monday, find him and pull him into one of our old snogging hideaways and tell him that I did believe in him and trust him to be a nice guy. The trouble was, that wasn't true.

It was uberdrip Lewis who told me that Jonah would be at the Moth Ball on Friday night. We found ourselves sitting together in the waiting area outside the school secretary's office. I was there first, quite enjoying the dark silence and soft leather chairs that they'd installed to make any parents who might have to wait there think the school was quite posh. The main building, where the chief admin staff worked, still looked like the Victorian grammar school it had once been, while all the newer buildings were thin and plasticky, painted in various horrible greys and beiges.

Lewis lurched up, his trainers squeaking on the polished wooden floor, and sat down, sighing a lot. At first, he didn't seem to have recognised me, or convincingly pretended that he hadn't. He did the self-conscious things people do when they're sort of nervous, rummaging through his bag, changing position too much, humming. I tried not to look at him, pretending that I hadn't recognised him because I'd been preoccupied.

'Ah, I didn't see it was you!' he said suddenly. 'What you doing here?' I told him (boring thing about updating my mum's work contact details) and he told me (boring thing about moving outside school catchment area). He asked me how long I'd been waiting and I said a tiny girl with cornrows had gone in about ten minutes before, and I'd been waiting about ten minutes before that. After that, we both started rummaging in our bags again and I wondered if we'd be able to get away with not saying anything else until it was my turn to go in.

'You going to this Halloween thing, then?' Lewis said.

'No.' This seemed rudely abrupt, so I had to come up with something else. 'You?'

'Yeah, we're all going.'

'Are you dressing up?' I asked.

'Well, Steve was trying to get us all to go as something blasphemous, but Jonah and he had a fight about it, so now we're not quite sure.'

'They had a fight?'

'Nothing big. I mean, they've been a bit . . . off with each other recently.'

'Jonah's not going, though, so why does he care what Steve's wearing?'

'Yeah, he is going,' Lewis said.

'Oh, right,' I said, embarrassed. It had only been a few days since Jonah and I had broken up, so I felt as though nothing he was doing should be surprising to me yet.

'He's maybe only just got a ticket, I think,' Lewis said, as if he felt and understood the embarrassment. He scratched his pale, freckled nose. ''Cause when we were planning what to wear we didn't talk about a costume for Jonah. I think I thought that was because he was going with you, so wouldn't be coming with us, so wouldn't be wearing what we were wearing, or whatever.'

'Lewis, can I ask you something?'

'Yeah?'

'Why would you want to go in blasphemous costumes, knowing you'd upset people or offend them?'

'It's just funny,' Lewis said, shrugging.

'But you could get in trouble with the school, couldn't you?'

'Dunno.'

'Is this all about pissing people off?'

'Course not!' Lewis said. 'Well, I don't know. For Steve it is, Dom just likes being outrageous, it gives him a kick.'

'What about Jonah?'

Lewis shrugged again. I slightly wanted to slap him. I was feeling weird and energised, realising that my heart was making decisions and my brain hadn't caught up with them yet. I had to go to the Halloween party and see all of this play out. *Make him nice*, Sam had told me. I didn't know if I could do that. I'm pretty sure I wasn't that nice myself. But I couldn't just carry on wishing for him and with my heart beating only for him and with him not knowing anything about it. Even if I just stared at him and hoped he'd read my mind and it didn't work and I went home alone, I had to do something to let him know I'd come back for him. I had to be there.

Chapter 13

The Joker is nervous. He has a small flat bottle of vodka held within the elastic of his underwear. There's a cradle of masking tape around it to stop it falling. But how careful are the searches going to be? He might get sent home. But it looks like it's just bags and coats. Joker hands his coat over and smiles at Catwoman as they hold hands again and walk in together. They find their friends, a Batman and a Riddler.

The Devil, a nun and Jesus are looking out of an upper-floor window, rating the sexiness of all the girls heading towards the building. Three girls get the thumbs up: a zombie Dorothy from *The Wizard of Oz*, Marilyn Monroe swinging a bag stuffed with fake sleeping pills, and Eve, as in the first woman. Marilyn Monroe gets delayed for a long time in the bag search.

A handsome priest steps off the bus, runs his hand

through his shiny black hair and fiddles with his dog collar. His heart is beating as he heads towards the school, but he's not sure why. His phone chirps with a text.

We're upstairs. Come n find us.

He's disappointed.

Zombie Michael Jackson, Elvis, Sid Vicious, and a John Lennon with an oozing bullet hole are dancing together downstairs in the main party area. They nudge each other when the priest comes in, but keep dancing. One of the dead rock stars clicks his tongue and rolls his eyes, yelling next to his friend's ear so his joke can be heard above the music. When *Thriller* comes on, they cheer. All the dancers in the room try to do the right moves, and some are better than others, but this is the first song of the night that gets everyone there really excited, with the dance floor jam-packed in seconds. The building throbs in time with the music and the stamping and jumping. It's a full house tonight.

Some teachers with whitened faces and black eyeliner stand in a group by the entrance, making funny remarks about the costumes as they come in, laughing at their own jokes, being a bit ruder than they usually would be to pupils. The pupils are a lot ruder than they usually would be back. This makes the teachers laugh even more loudly. They take it in turns to go off in twos to check everyone is behaving – one of the pair goes upstairs, the other stays down and does the circuit, weaving through the dance floor to the kitchen, where those people with tokens are swapping them for two weak alcoholic drinks and water is forced on anyone who looks a bit tired. It's a school party, after all.

The priest goes upstairs and finds the Devil, Jesus and the nun. He sticks around to talk to them as they carry on looking out of the window, but he's leaning over the balcony on the other side, looking into the main hall where people come through on their way to the dance floor. There's a big staircase connecting this balcony to the ground floor, and it's already covered with snogging couples. It looks mad: werewolf hands groping a vampire virgin in a long white nightdress, a naughty witch getting off with an unmasked Spiderman.

'I am soooo having a piece of Marilyn Monroe,' says the nun.

'You lesbian,' says the Devil.

The priest turns round. He gives a hollow laugh. 'You haven't got a chance,' the priest says. 'That's Ian's sister's mate. They think we're dicks.'

'Nah, she looked at me,' the nun says. 'I know that look.'

'Think you might be sticking to that vow of celibacy a bit longer than you think, Sister,' says the Devil. Everyone laughs except the priest.

A couple of hours later and everyone is louder, or kissing. The Joker and Catwoman are kissing and drinking his vodka in the small stock cupboard behind the kitchen, where they have gone under the pretext of getting another box of crisps.

'You look so beautiful,' Joker says. 'You're the most beautiful girl here tonight.'

'Hardly,' says Catwoman. 'You saw Eve, didn't you?' Joker smiles. 'All right, all right!' Catwoman says. 'You don't have to look so delighted by the memory!'

'She's not like you,' Joker says. 'You're naturally beautiful. She's all fake eyelashes and bleach and bra padding.'

'Meow!' says Catwoman, and he laughs and kisses her.

The nun and Marilyn are giggling together. The Devil is leaning closer to Eve than Eve would like and agreeing loudly with things he thinks she's said (but she hasn't, really), while staring hard at her chest. She's looking past him over the balcony for zombie Dorothy, and wishing she'd stayed with her. Jesus is looking around quite desperately, too, as if he would rather be anywhere else in the world. He has taken off his beard, and his face looks tired and childlike. He catches the eye of Michael Jackson and starts slightly. Michael Jackson seems to spot the fear and a few minutes later, the dead rock stars have moved closer to the blasphemers and the two groups can hear each other.

'Oh, that's brave,' says Michael Jackson loudly to his friends. 'It's really brave. I wonder why they didn't attack any Muslim figures, given that they seem to have such a problem with Islam.'

The nun breaks away from Marilyn. 'Why do you think?' he says, talking directly to Michael Jackson now.

Michael Jackson raises one eyebrow. 'Why don't you tell me?'

The priest has been to the bathroom, and taken his time getting back to his friends, because he had nothing to say to them and didn't want to hear anything they said either. He's been hanging around downstairs for a while, leaning against the wall by the dance floor with his eyes closed, feeling the thrum thrum of the music, like a motorbike revving up somewhere down his spine. He doesn't notice how many girls are staring at him, particularly the younger ones, or realise how moody and beautiful he is, with his angsty fine-boned face. He's just thinking about the girl, one girl. His girl. But she's not his any more. He's hot and his collar is tight and he needs some air. He walks through to the entrance hall, looks up at the staircase that's messy with snogging couples smearing their waxy make-up on to each other's faces, and he spots his friends, still on the balcony, not joining the real party. They look stupid. And he looks stupid for agreeing to dress like them. It's pathetic. No one is shocked, they're just stuck telling the same bad joke all night.

Then he notices they're squaring up to the dead rock stars. The nun is getting in Michael Jackson's face, pointing at him with an aggressive finger. The priest wants to just leave them to it, but he knows he has to stop them. He thinks about the girl, and how she'd want him to stop them. As he pictures her face he forgets to breathe, and his brain starts chattering with excitement and sadness and love that's so fierce it frightens him. He runs up the stairs as fast as he can, accidentally kicking a snogging person in the leg and treading on another one's cape.

The Joker is watching the boys on the balcony, too – he's waiting for Catwoman to finish chatting with her friends. He's the level of drunk that makes him feel good about himself now, and he thinks it'd be a good idea if he stepped in and told all the guys arguing upstairs to chill out. So he heads towards the stairs too, making the kissers even angrier, so that some of them stop kissing and press themselves against the edges of the staircase to let him through, while swearing at him.

Finding themselves together, they stop at the top, the priest and the Joker, and look at each other. They are very close.

'You're on your own this evening, Father?' the Joker says, and he can't keep the smile off his face or out of his voice. The last time he met the priest, he was scared, although he didn't admit that to anyone. This evening he's not scared at all. He's even angry that he was ever scared. The priest looks pathetic, smaller and stranger, as if he hasn't slept in a month and he'll scream like a girl if you shout at him.

'You're a bit too interested in my love life, aren't you?' says the priest. 'Oh, but I forgot – you're still a bit obsessed with my girlfriend.'

'Wow, is this what they call denial?' says the Joker. 'From what I heard she doesn't want anything to do with you. She thinks you're scum.'

The priest reddens and bites the inside of his cheek. He has nothing, he can't even be sure of being able to talk right now.

'And of course I'm not obsessed with her,' the Joker says. 'Because, unlike you, I've got a girlfriend. But yeah, I think it's fair to say your ex is still very interested . . . in my *advice*.'

The Joker's head snaps back when the priest punches him. The girls on the stairs who are closest to them scream, while a ghost near the top of the stairs swears at the Joker for standing on his girlfriend's hand and kneeing her in the face as he stumbles. When he regains his footing, the Joker grabs hold of the priest's throat, and his dog-collar scrunches and flicks out of the shirt. The snoggers on the stairs start getting up and trying to squeeze past them up to the balcony. The priest's friends and the dead rock stars start to head over in case they're needed, as the priest and the Joker start gripping and hitting each other.

The nun shouts at the priest to stop. The Devil and Michael Jackson reach the staircase at the same time, elbowing each other to be first to help. The Joker's spine curls back horribly over the banister with the priest's hand under his chin. Eve screams for them to stop. Michael Jackson grabs the priest's arm and he topples backwards so they both fall over. The Joker stands heavily on the priest's leg as he tries to steady himself, but as the priest fights to stand again, shoving him back, the Joker is unbalanced, the banister clunks out of position, and the Joker falls over the staircase. They watch helplessly as he drops like a pile of clothes, there is a sickening smothered crack, and the side of his head hits the floor below.

When Alice arrives at the bag check area, she sees the last of the teachers running in a panic into the main hall. For a moment she's frozen by confusion, but she can tell something very bad is happening. She runs after him.

Chapter 14

The first time I saw a film version of *Alice in Wonderland* I was very young and off school with German measles and I kept falling asleep, and after I'd seen it I wondered how much of it had been a dream. Years later I saw it again, the same one, and it made me tingly inside, as if part of my childhood had been imprisoned inside it and I could glimpse it while the film was on. I used to read the book over and over, and I thought it was amazing, but it was that strange film of it that seemed magical to me, the real *Alice in Wonderland*.

So it had to be Alice. But I could hardly go to a Halloween party looking that cute. The Alice outfit was easy to make – I already had a full-skirted blue summer dress that had felt a bit too girly for me to wear normally. I put it over a short-sleeved white school shirt, and got some net underskirts from the market to puff it out, and customised a white apron and sewed it in place. Then I smeared the apron with fake blood and daubed the blood all over a white furry toy rabbit and cut it into two pieces.

I'd started straightening my hair almost as soon as I got home from school and I finished it off with a black Alice band. I picked up the hacked-apart rabbit and my big plastic bowie knife. I did look cute, I thought. But funny, too. For a moment, the pleasure of wearing clothes I liked myself in and feeling pretty allowed me to shut out reality. I had half lost my friends – I hadn't told them I'd bought a ticket and planned to go. My boyfriend had dumped me. For some reason I'd honestly believed I could just turn up alone, snap on the fake confidence force field, and ... And then what? Get the boyfriend back? The friends? There was no way I could walk into a party of mostly sixth-formers in my little girl dress. You know how you wake up from a dream in which you've had a brilliant idea – like you've written a song or solved a problem – and you start trying to piece together the idea from what you remember, and suddenly you realise it's rubbish, and it falls apart like a handful of sand.

I put the bunny down gently as if he was real and hurt, and stroked his decapitated head. I got my hand smeared in the fake blood on my apron, and wiped it off lower down. I looked ridiculous. I took a big bag of crisps out of the cupboard and sat down in front of *EastEnders*.

Paul walked in. 'What time are you going?' he said. He stared at me too long, then said, 'There's a very old non-cartoon version of *Alice* with an actress called Fiona Fullerton as Alice, and with your hair straight, you look like her.'

I stared at him open-mouthed. 'That's the version I like.'

'Really?' Paul said. It felt like there was more to say, a real conversation ready to go, but we were trapped by the fact that we'd always been enemies. 'What time are your friends coming?'

'Er . . .' I was embarrassed. 'They're not. I was going to walk round by myself.' I braced myself for him asking why.

'Oh, okay,' Paul said. 'I can walk round with you, if you like. I mean, 'cause it's dark and that. Don't worry, I'll come back before anyone sees me.'

'It's only two minutes away,' I said. 'You'd be coming back by the end of our street.'

'That's okay, though . . .' He tapped his pockets a bit nervously. 'Anyway, let me know.' He went through to the kitchen. I ate some crisps. He came back in. 'You are going, aren't you?'

I shrugged. 'Maybe not, dunno if I feel like it.'

'Well, be a waste of your outfit.' Paul turned to go

again, and then stopped and turned back. 'When are you going to get a chance to be Alice again?'

He went back into the kitchen. I was worried he was going to tell my mum that I wasn't going and she was going to come in straight away and make a big deal about everything, and I sighed and decided to just go to bed. Then I heard Paul asking my mum if we had any garlic, then they were talking about spaghetti, and that was that.

I went to my bedroom and looked at myself in the mirror again, with my straight hair and thick black eyeliner. I didn't look anything like me. I looked the way I always hoped I'd look when I looked in a mirror, before seeing the disappointing reality. I didn't know what would happen if I went, but I knew what would happen if I didn't go.

'I'm going to go now,' I said, looking into the kitchen, where my mum and Paul were reading a newspaper together, my mum standing behind Paul and resting her head on his shoulder.

'You've got your phone?' said my mum.

'Yeah.'

'I'll just pop out with you, eh?' said Paul, reaching out for his shoes with his toes.

'Um. Sure,' I said.

I could hear the music from the party before we reached the gates.

'Obviously if you're walking home with a friend, that's fine,' Paul said. 'But don't walk home alone, you know your mum worries.'

I didn't say anything.

'Listen,' Paul went on. 'I know I'm not a member of the family. I don't expect to be. It's you and your mum and I'm the weirdo bloke who hangs around annoying you . . .'

I wondered why he was talking this way. I guessed that my mum had had a word with him, since our weird needy hug on the night I didn't really sleep with Jonah. 'It's really not like that . . .' I hoped he wouldn't keep talking. It was me and my mum who needed to sort things out, not me and Paul.

'I know that, and I don't mind. I don't mind being a guest of the O'Neills and not one of them. It may look like she's not on your side, but it's because she's embarrassed about being so much on your side that she has to stick up for me sometimes.'

'But she should be on my side,' I said, like a five year old.

Paul smiled. 'She would kick my ass if she thought it amused you,' he said.

We couldn't really see things so differently, could we? I knew her better, I knew best, but if he believed that – really believed it – maybe I didn't know everything.

'Okay, Alice, I'm going to make like the Cheshire

Cat before any of your friends see me. Have a good time.'

It was a freezing cold night, but I didn't feel cold. I couldn't really feel anything, except that it was a bit unreal walking into the part of school where I'm not allowed, wearing a funny little dress, holding two halves of a toy rabbit. I was holding the ticket in my hand so I didn't lose it.

As I pushed open the double doors the sudden warmth prickled my cheeks. There was a really loud clang that made me jump as a chair got pushed over, and I could see Mr Travis, my history teacher from Year 9, running through into the main hall. There was no one around to check my ticket or tell me where to leave my coat, and it gave me a weird feeling. I started to run.

There was a crowd, getting bigger all the time, and people shouting. The first person I saw was Nashriq halfway down the main stairs, dressed as Michael Jackson. In the middle of the crowd I could see Isobel, in her zombie Dorothy costume, and she was crying, in a way I'd never seen her crying before, maybe never seen anyone crying before. Really screaming, as if she was in pain. Sophie was next to her, with her arm around Isobel. I reacted slowly, confused, and I remember I even had time to look Sophie up and down and feel stupidly jealous of her beautiful body in the shiny catsuit, before I saw Ian. He was lying flat in front of them and one of the teachers was carefully pressing rolled-up jackets and jumpers around his neck to try to keep him still. But he wasn't moving. His face was ghost white, covered in Joker make-up. His shirt was bloody. One of his legs was twisted in a way that seemed impossible, like a trick leg with nothing in the trousers. It made me want to throw up.

I shouted, 'IAN!' trying to make my way through the people, and Jonah heard me and looked up. We were staring at each other, frozen to the spot, while around us kids jostled and pushed and shouted, and then there were sirens and an ambulance and police and they took Ian and Jonah away. Isobel and Sophie went with Ian. I didn't go with anyone, and I felt that people could see how useless and disconnected I was, and would laugh at me.

I saw Finian and a nun talking to a policeman. I'd known she was going as Marilyn Monroe but it took me a while to realise the nun was Steve. The only person I could get to was Josette, who was sitting on the floor in a flesh-coloured body stocking covered with sewn-on leaves, crying into her mobile. I asked her what had happened but she didn't seem to hear me. I could hear people asking if Ian was dead and saying he was definitely not dead and saying he was definitely dead. Under the strip lighting everyone's streaked make-up and badly made costumes looked horrible. I guess mine did too. Lewis was sitting on his own, scared and close to tears in a long white robe and Jesus sandals.

I called home. Paul was there in minutes.

Two months later

I heard that Isobel's dad was suing the school but I don't know if it's true. I didn't ask Ian about it, anyway, when he finally let me come and visit him, a few days after Christmas.

'It's not as bad as it looks,' he said. One of his legs was hooked up in traction, with pulleys and strings and weights tied to it. His arms were in plaster, and around his head there was a big collar thing with fat metal rods sticking from it into blood-crusted holes in his forehead and shoulders.

I wanted to cry, but I wouldn't let myself. I knew if I did, Ian would feel sorry for me and try to make me feel better, the way he always had when I'd cried during our fights. He had the right to hate me as much as he liked and I wasn't going to interfere with that. I clenched my teeth together hard.

'I brought you a book,' I said. 'But that seems pretty stupid, given . . .'

'No, I can hold books fine,' Ian said. He took it from me with tiny fingertips poking out from his plastered arm. 'It looks good.'

'It's stupid, sorry,' I said.

'No,' Ian said, trying less hard.

'You must hate me. I know I don't have any right to be here.'

188

'I don't hate you. It's not your fault.'

'Well, whether it's my fault or not, you must hate me.'

'Cassidy —'

'You must hate him.'

'Do *you*?' Ian asked.

'YES,' I said. I sat down on the chair next to the bed. 'Of course I do. I can't believe he didn't have to go to prison.'

'It was just a fight,' Ian said. 'He wasn't trying to kill me. Look, it's done now.'

'Are you going to be okay?'

'Yes.'

'Isobel said you might not be.'

'Isobel's just worried. I don't blame you, Cassidy.'

'But I do.' I started biting my nails. 'And I blame you.'

'Well, I shouldn't have got involved, you're right. But it was still the right thing to do, because it turned out you didn't really know what you were doing.'

I got angry before I could help it. 'No, I mean, I blame you for breaking up with me. I know how stupid that sounds. But that's where it all started.'

'Well, you're right that that sounds stupid.' We sat there, both angry, me knowing I had no right to be.

'I just wish you hadn't made everything different,' I whispered.

'And if I hadn't?'

'Well, I'm not saying you'd have been happy, but none of this —'

'Rubbish,' Ian said. 'We were bored with each other. You would have seen Jonah and run off with him if I hadn't moved first.'

'That's not true,' I said. 'I miss you.'

'No,' Ian said. 'You miss the old *you*, and the place we were in where you didn't have to think about what happened from one day to the next.'

I knew what he was saying was true. I think I wanted him to believe he had made all the choices, though, so that he wouldn't blame me. That he'd started everything going in the wrong direction.

'How's Sophie?'

'Sophie's great,' Ian said, nodding, and his eyes smiled at the thought of her. That still hurt. 'Look, Cassidy, I'm not about to tell you something good will come from this, because I have spikes in my head and I have to ask for help peeing, but we *have changed*. You are not the girl who was my girlfriend, and you shouldn't want to be. You'll find a better guy than me. For one thing, you'll find someone who loves you.' It was a cruel thing to say, and I was happy to take it.

'I don't care about boyfriends,' I said. 'Do you really think I'm miserable because you're not my boyfriend and I haven't got a boyfriend?'

'I don't have any claim on knowing what you think any more,' Ian said. 'But you need to know that I'm not angry with you. I don't blame you. And I want you to be okay.'

I wasn't sure how much of that was true. He was angry about something and he was angry with someone, and it was hard to believe I didn't qualify. But I was beginning to realise that I'd gone to visit him to make myself feel better – whether that came from seeing he was okay, or from having him forgive me, or from soaking up some of his anger because I thought I needed punishing. Maybe I hoped he'd tell Isobel how sorry I was and she'd start speaking to me again. One thing I was not doing was making Ian feel better, and that wasn't right.

I saw Sophie on my way out, hiding behind the drinks machine, waiting for me to leave and hoping I wouldn't spot her. She didn't want to confront me or make me feel guilty. Ian was going to be fine. He had already found his better girl.

I went round to Sam's house in the afternoon.

'You can't stay,' he said, excitedly, as he sped down the hall into his bedroom. 'But come and sit down now, I have to show you something.'

He pulled up an email on his computer screen. He had emailed: *Got Fortress of the Serpent for Christmas. Any good?*

The reply went: *It is X-L-ENT. Already played the*

demo. Any chance u can bring it round l8r? Rashad.

'He does text-speak in his emails,' I said.

'Oh, shut up,' Sam said. 'That's how people younger than you talk.'

I growled at him because I couldn't shove him hard, like he deserved.

'So, is it a date?'

'Of course it's not,' Sam said. 'And you're wrong if you think that's what I want. He's just my mate.' He gave me a wide, gorgeous smile, and his eyes were sad for so short a time that I almost thought I'd imagined it. 'Did you have a good Christmas?'

'It wasn't bad,' I said. 'You know, considering I don't have any friends except you, I had to sit through *the* most awkward Boxing Day of all time with my dad's *other* family, and my mum gave me a warm coat for Christmas . . .'

'A *nice* warm coat?'

'You've just seen it.'

'Oh, that. Yeah, that *is* a nice coat,' Sam said, with a smirk.

'Isn't it?' I said, smiling. 'But Paul gave me my own tiny laptop. He said he's sick of me snooping around in his browsing history to check on the academic sites he's visited.'

'Really?'

'He was joking.'

'What do you think?' Sam asked. 'You've been a bit hard on him?'

'If he thinks he can buy me off with cool stuff . . . well, I can live with that.'

When I got home I booted up my tiny, new, powder-blue laptop and checked my messages. There was one from Jonah, as there was every day, but it didn't have any text today, just a song. I clicked it open. An Ella Fitzgerald track: 'What Are You Doing New Year's Eve?' I hadn't realised it was New Year's Eve the next day. I wouldn't be doing anything, I wanted to tell him, but I hadn't replied to a single one of Jonah's emails since Halloween. He'd moved to the sixth-form college in town and I didn't see him around even accidentally, but the emails still came. Sometimes short ones, sometimes long ones – I felt worse ignoring those. When the song ended I felt sad and played it again, but I didn't reply.

It's New Year's Eve today, and I'm not doing anything.

I went out this morning to buy my mum her newspaper and it started to snow. I tilted my head up to the sky to watch it falling – it makes you dizzy and is impossibly, amazingly beautiful that way – and when I looked forward again, Jonah was standing there in front of me.

'Don't run away,' he said. I just shook my head and turned away, pulling my nice coat more closely around myself. 'Cassidy. *Cassidy.*' But then I stood there with my back to him, unable to go. 'I . . .' He sighed. 'I know you don't want to see me now.' I focused on the snow melting on my sleeves. 'You can't know how much it kills me to think of that night,' Jonah said. 'I would do anything to make it not have happened.'

'You've told me all this,' I said. 'And I believe you.'

'I love you.'

'You've told me that too.'

'But you don't care?'

'No,' I said. 'I don't care.' So easy to say something like this and make it believable, to sound all dead and flat. I dropped the newspaper as I started to walk away, and when I picked it up I could feel the imprint of my fist, I'd been gripping it so hard.

'When I think,' Jonah said, 'that you have completely and totally stopped loving me, I'll leave you alone.'

'You're so sure I ever loved you?' I said.

Jonah smiled. 'I have to believe you still do.'

Maybe he'll get tired of waiting before I'm ready to take him back, and maybe I'll be sad if that happens. I'd be there to watch it, him letting me go – I've already applied to the sixth-form college for next year, the one Jonah transferred to. I don't want to do another two years of Samuel Bond's with the same people I've always gone to school with, all of them knowing what I'm like – what I *was* like.

Jonah's right: I still love him. That's not enough, though. I'm going to take Sam's advice, but I have to try to make *me* nice first. I need to start listening and reading and thinking, so that I can never be fooled or seduced or frightened by the wrong people again. So I can step up when things don't feel right. I want to be able to trust myself. If Jonah's prepared to wait for me, I want to be worth the wait.

Also by Kate le Vann

Tessa
in
Love

Wolfie was totally scruffy . . . and totally sexy. It wasn't love at first sight, because I'd been aware of him for years and just hadn't noticed before. It was like really seeing someone for the first time.

Tessa has always been 'the quiet one', while her best friend, Matty, is outgoing and constantly has boys flocking around her. But when Tessa falls in love for the first time at sixteen, everything changes. Tessa finds a soulmate in Wolfie, a committed green activist, and she grows more confident and outspoken every day. She also begins to look at the world differently . . .

But just when their love is at its strongest, tragedy strikes. How will she ever be able to cope?

'A fabulous story – I couldn't put it down.'
Wendy Cooling, children's books consultant

Things I Know About Love

*1. People don't always tell you the truth
about how they feel.
2. Nothing that happens between two people is
guaranteed to be private.
3. I don't know if you ever get over having
your heart broken.*

Livia's experience of love has been disappointing, to say
the least. But all that is about to change. After years of
illness, she's off to spend the summer with her brother
in America. She's making up for lost time, and she's
writing it all down in her private blog.

America is everything she'd dreamed of –
and then she meets Adam. Can Livia put the past
behind her and risk falling in love again?

'Compelling, poignant and uplifting . . . Kate's writing is
perfectly pitched.' Claudia Mody, Waterstones

Two Friends, One Summer

Best friends Samantha and Rachel are spending the holidays with two families in France. They're used to doing everything together, but suddenly they're living in different worlds.

Rachel's family is glamorous, vivacious and right in the centre of everything, but Samantha is stuck with a strict family who live in the middle of nowhere.

Samantha is shaken – she's used to being the outgoing one, and now their roles are reversed. As new experiences and boys threaten the trust between her and Rachel, it looks unlikely that their lifelong friendship can survive this turbulent summer . . .

'Sweet and insightful.' Mizz

RAIN

I remember Sarah. She was funny and happy and her voice went croaky when she was excited. I loved her more than anything. But she died before I ever really knew her: she was twenty-six. She was my mother.

Rain Lindsay is spending her first summer away from her father at her grandmother's house in London.

London is scary and exciting – just like Harry, a student who is helping her grandmother renovate the house. Slowly their suspicion of each other lessens as Harry helps Rain discover more about her dead mother, whose diary Rain finds in her old bedroom. A diary that contains unsettling secrets . . .

An utterly compelling story of a girl on the brink of love and adulthood.

'This is compelling reading, utterly, painfully believable, painstakingly and movingly charted.'
BOOKS FOR KEEPS

www.piccadillypress.co.uk

☆ The latest news on forthcoming books

☆ Chapter previews

☆ Author biographies

☆ Fun quizzes

☆ Reader reviews

☆ Competitions and fab prizes

☆ Book features and cool downloads

☆ And much, much more . . .

Log on and check it out!

Piccadilly Press